"W

Lloyd stared [...] eyes, trying to read her mind. He suspected she was assessing where they were now and where they might be in the future. He was doing the same thing in his head. In that moment he realized that neither of them was cut out for one-night stands, even though their relationship had more or less started that way.

"Do you want the truth?" She held his gaze as she asked the question.

"Yeah. I think I can handle it," he said.

"I'm thinking I really like you. And I haven't said that to anyone in a long time...." She looked away then and he wondered if she would shy away now, afraid that she'd revealed too much.

"The feeling is mutual," he said. After that, Courtney's gaze focused on his mouth and he could feel her reserve slipping away....

Books by Devon Vaughn Archer

Kimani Romance

Christmas Heat
Destined to Meet

DEVON VAUGHN ARCHER

Devon had the distinction of becoming the first male to write solo for Harlequin's Arabesque line with the groundbreaking 2006 contemporary romance *Love Once Again*. Devon's first romance novel, *Dark and Dashing*, appeared in the 2005 two-for-one volume *Slow Motion*, which received four and a half stars from *Romantic Times BOOKreviews*.

Devon lives in the Pacific Northwest with his beautiful wife, Loraine, and is busy working on his next Kimani Romance. Devon encourages fan feedback and can be e-mailed at RBarri@RBarriFlowers.com.

Destined to MEET

devon vaughn archer

KIMANI ROMANCE

KIMANI PRESS™

ISBN-13: 978-0-373-86071-5
ISBN-10:   0-373-86071-4

DESTINED TO MEET

www.kimanipress.com

Printed in U.S.A.

Dear Reader,

After a night of steamy passion is marred by a hit-and-run tragedy, Courtney Hudson and Lloyd Vance must deal with loss while finding their way back to each other. The journey is a less-than-smooth ride as a criminal investigation and trust issues threaten to ruin the strides made and what seems to be Courtney and Lloyd's destiny of a lifetime together in love. But can anything truly stand in the way of two people who are meant to be together?

If you believe some things are simply destiny at work, then you will find this novel a heartwarming love story that stays with you well after reading the final page.

I invite readers to visit my page at MySpace, www.myspace.com/devonvaughnarcher.
Also visit my blog at Romance Sirens: www.romancesirens.com/devon-vaughn-archer.

All the best,

Devon Vaughn Archer

To the love of my life, H. Loraine, who always has a twinkle in her eyes and took the journey with me into a world of romance and being there for each other across the span of time.

For Mom, Jackie and her girls, and my female friends who enjoy romance fiction.

I also dedicate this book to my growing legion of fans who enthusiastically keep coming back for more and inspiring me to continue to deliver exciting, romantic and sensual love stories time and time again.

Chapter 1

Lloyd Vance made his way around the crowded club, exchanging a few words with familiar faces, and generally wondering what the hell he was doing there. He wasn't the type to hang out in bars, preferring a mellower atmosphere, even staying home and watching TV on a Friday night. But he was in a new city and just trying to fit in as best he could.

Never mind that the person he was supposed to meet had called to say he wasn't coming after all. Maybe that should have been a clue to call it a night.

But Lloyd had never taken the easy route, even when he chose to move to another state. At thirty-six, he was at a stage of his life where taking chances seemed a better bet than sticking with a career and a dismal personal life.

So here I am tonight, ready for a challenge.

Nursing a 007 martini, Lloyd spotted an attractive woman seated at a table alone. Was she really by herself? That seemed hard to fathom with all the men on the prowl for anyone wearing a skirt.

The lady is flat-out gorgeous. She reminded him of a cross between Alicia Keys and Tracee Ellis Ross—neither of whom he could go wrong with.

Wonder if she's up for some company? Only one way to find out….

Lloyd tasted his drink and headed in the lady's direction, unable to take his eyes off her. This could either be good or bad news, depending on which way the wind blew.

Courtney Hudson decided for once to live adventurously, if not dangerously. Three years after losing her husband, Joseph, in a freak accident, she was ready to let loose and put some passion back into her life.

Or at least try to accommodate her cousin Pilar, who had talked Courtney into checking out the hot new club in town, the Train Stop. According to Pilar, the place was supposed to be the cure-all for an attractive widow looking to get back in the game with some red-hot hunk who knew how to set the sheets on fire.

But Pilar had not bothered to show up or answer her cell phone, leaving Courtney to fend for herself.

I'm going to get you for this, Pilar, unless you've got a damn good reason for not showing.

She sipped on a Colorado Bulldog and listened to the Black Eyed Peas tune while checking out the hard bodies gyrating on the dance floor. It reminded Courtney of a time when she could move to the groove as well as anyone. That was before tragedy struck and the desire seemed to all but vanish.

This was probably a mistake. Maybe I should go. At thirty-three, I should find something better to do with my time than hang out at a club all by myself.

"Where is he?" The velvety deep voice with an inflection that Courtney couldn't quite place spoke bluntly from behind, ending her reverie.

Courtney jerked her head around and gazed directly into the deep pools of gray staring back. "Excuse me...?"

"I asked where is the jerk who would leave such a gorgeous woman sitting here counting heads?"

Courtney wasn't sure if he was serious or not, but she never had a problem with someone calling her gorgeous. A quick scan told her that the man wasn't bad himself. Quite the opposite. He was a dead ringer for Will Smith, which spoke for itself.

Was the actor making a movie in Lake Barri, Colorado, and taking a break by mingling with the locals?

Courtney decided that this man was taller and more muscular than Will without losing any of his drop-dead good-looking features, including the closely cropped, sharply lined raven hair.

"I'm here alone," she told him. No thanks to Pilar.

He grinned slowly, holding a cocktail. "Well, that explains it, and makes two of us. I was supposed to meet up with a buddy for a few drinks, but he backed out at the last moment."

"Join the club. My cousin seems to have strangely lost her way."

She's even lovelier up close. What I wouldn't give to run my fingers through that luscious, long brown-blond hair nestled across her shoulders.

Lloyd welcomed the fortuitous turn of events. "Their loss can definitely be our gain."

Courtney couldn't help but flash her smile at him. "Oh, you think so, do you?"

"Why not? We're two fish out of water, if I'm reading you correctly." She didn't strike him as the type to come to a club by herself very often. "Maybe the stars aligned on this night, and destiny shone down on us to get together."

Courtney laughed over her drink. "You don't really believe that, do you?"

He chuckled—a deep and sensual sound—making him that much more appealing. "No, not really. But I do know that when I saw you clear across the room, I had to come over here for a better look. And I'm glad I did."

Courtney smiled. *So am I, even if I'm having trouble buying that age-old, across-the-room line. Still beats pretending to be occupied. Not to mention he's easily the most handsome and sexiest man in the club.*

"Do you want to sit down?"

"Only if you don't want to get up and show them how it's done on the dance floor."

Though tempted, Courtney decided not to press her luck. "I'm not much of a dancer," she said as an excuse.

"Neither am I." He sat in the chair closest to hers. "My name's Lloyd."

"Courtney."

"Nice meeting you."

He stuck out his hand and she shook it, noting how strong his hands were. He smelled good, too. Was that Obsession he was wearing?

"You, too." Courtney had never met a Lloyd before. Or a man with such an appealing voice. Maybe he really was a fish out of water. "Something tells me you're not from around here."

Am I that obvious? He cracked a half smile. "Something would be right. I'm from Anchorage."

"As in Alaska?"

"Born and raised there," he said matter-of-factly.

Her gold-flecked ebony eyes widened. "Interesting…"

Lloyd ran long fingers across his taut jawline. "I know, the 'last-frontier' state isn't the first to come to mind for an oak-skinned man." He tasted the drink. "Not as unusual as it might seem. My old man was stationed there in the military. He married an Alaskan native, and they had me."

"How did you end up in Lake Barri?" Courtney sipped her cocktail and hoped she wasn't being too inquisitive. "It's pretty far from home."

Lloyd met her eyes. "That's an easy one. My job brought me here two months ago. I'm still getting settled in, but it's getting better all the time."

Courtney flushed under the weight of his gaze. "That's good to hear," she managed.

"I think so." He sat back. "So tell me something about you."

She sighed, always finding this the hardest part in exchanging information with a new person. "Well, I'm a widow, a children's book author and I grew up here."

Lloyd focused in on the first part of that. "You're pretty young to be a widow, aren't you?"

"I know," Courtney said thoughtfully. "But sometimes things happen that we can't do anything about."

Lloyd scratched his nose. "You're right about that. All any of us can do is live for today."

How about tonight? "I can't argue with that."

"Then you're a wiser person than most, who tend to cling to the past as though there were no other choice."

"That's not me." Courtney was through wishing her life had turned out differently, especially her husband's death. It was time to take life by the horns and charge ahead.

"Children's books, huh?" Lloyd asked, curiosity piqued. He wondered if she had any kids.

Courtney nodded. "Actually I write middle-grade fiction. I've had ten books published to date."

"I'm impressed. Never met an author before."

"Trust me, it's not as glamorous as you might think. Writing is hard work, and for most of us it's not about the money, but the joy of publishing quality material that the readers can appreciate."

"Well put." He sipped his drink and admired the woman who turned him on like crazy. "Beauty, talent and a proper perspective. Can't ask for much more than that."

Flattery just might get you everywhere. "So what job brought you from Alaska to Colorado?"

Lloyd paused. "I'm a cop—a detective, actually." *Hope that doesn't cause the train we seem to be on to derail.*

"Never met a cop before, so it looks like we're both charting new waters tonight."

He grinned, raising his glass. "I'll drink to that."

She hoisted her own glass for a phantom toast. "How long have you been in law enforcement?"

"Ten years. It's had its share of good and bad times. When the opportunity arose for a higher rank I went for it, deciding the time was right for me to move on."

"Any regrets?" Courtney looked at him inquisitively while wondering if *she* could be so courageous as to leave her comfort zone for a place thousands of miles away.

"Nope. Certainly not right now, anyway."

He gave her an "I want you" look, and Courtney felt a tingle like she hadn't in some time, as the feeling was mutual.

"In that case, I wish you well in Lake Barri."

"Thanks." Lloyd leaned forward. "Do you want to go somewhere that's not so loud and crowded?"

She lifted a brow demurely. "Where did you have in mind?"

"How about my place...or yours? Whatever you prefer."

Courtney had butterflies but still refused to settle back into her conservative nature. Not tonight. Especially since it was obvious that Pilar had no intention of showing up at the last minute to possibly thwart the plans.

"Your place sounds good."

His mouth curved up into a generous smile as if he couldn't wait one moment. "Let's go."

She looked at him. "Just one more thing, can I see your badge or ID?"

Lloyd nodded understandingly. "Of course."

He pulled out his police identification and allowed her to peruse it until completely satisfied that he was the real deal.

Courtney couldn't believe she was about to—in all likelihood—engage in a one-night stand. She had never gone that route before. But she hadn't met a man like Lloyd who could hold her attention since Joseph died.

Since they were still one-name strangers, with no reason to look ahead, Courtney promised to be content and enjoy whatever Lloyd brought to the table—or bed—without looking for more than he might be willing to give. Or that she wanted to offer.

As soon as they entered his house, Courtney felt Lloyd's sure hands all over her. Or was it the other way around? Whatever the case, she wasn't complaining, wanting to go the distance and experience what her body craved—and his clearly did, as well.

She cupped Lloyd's face and brought it down to hers, kissing his lips passionately, feeling his equally heated response. Courtney put her tongue in his mouth and tasted a combination of his drink and potent masculinity. She continued to explore, wanting to discover everything magical there was between his lips.

Lloyd seemed determined to match her, covering Courtney's mouth with his own, feverishly flattening, nibbling, sucking and exploring.

The kiss left Courtney breathless and when Lloyd began caressing her nipples through her thin top with his thumbs, she wanted to explode.

His erection bulged through his twill pants and pressed against her, leaving Courtney little doubt of his overpowering desire. She was just as eager to feel him inside her body.

"Do you have protection?" she murmured inside his mouth.

"Sure do," he responded huskily.

"Then let's not wait any longer!"

"Let's not!"

Courtney dove further into the kiss while her hands wandered across his hard body. Lloyd scooped her into his arms without breaking their lip lock. They bumped into things en route to his bedroom, intently focused on each other.

Ripping off their clothes till naked, they fell onto the

bed and resumed kissing. Courtney's heart pounded erratically as Lloyd slid his hand between her legs and began to stimulate her. She nearly came on the spot but fought the urge till they could climax together.

She grabbed hold of his hand and stopped it, unable to stand the burning sensations leaving her hot and very bothered.

"Make love to me, Lloyd."

"With pleasure."

Lloyd slipped on a condom. He positioned himself between Courtney's spread legs and drove in hard and deep. Without breaking the rhythm, he played with her breasts, which were full and pleasing, then kissed and nibbled her nipples, enjoying her sweet taste.

Courtney arched her back and urged him in even deeper, feeling his fullness igniting her nerve endings, starting the beginning stages of a climax. She attacked Lloyd's mouth with her own and heard a primal sound come from between them, and braced herself for what she knew would be an earth-shattering mutual explosion.

Lloyd shook as his powerful release came in waves. He felt Courtney tighten around him with her own orgasm, and winced when she clawed his back. He took a final deep breath before collapsing onto the bed.

He couldn't remember sex being this good or intense. Was it the same for her?

Courtney propped up on an elbow and kissed his shoulder. "Welcome to Lake Barri." *I can't believe I was so bold.*

Lloyd played with her hair. "Glad to be here and to get to know you."

Courtney felt a little self-conscious. "So does that mean you actually *want* to get to know me?" She couldn't assume anything these days, not when so many men seemed only interested in themselves.

He smiled and kissed her. "Yes, I'd like that."

"I think I would, too."

The ringing of a cell phone gave Lloyd a start. It was his. *Damn.* His first thought was to ignore it, but that wasn't part of the job description.

"I need to get that," he said reluctantly, and slid away from her. He stood and grabbed the cell phone off the nightstand. "Vance..."

Lloyd Vance. Courtney liked the sound of that. She had a mind to give Pilar a call. Maybe by now she was available. *And exactly what would I tell her? That I was in the bed of a man I just met?*

She smiled mischievously, imagining that Pilar, who could be quite adventurous herself when it came to men, would give her a thumbs-up.

Courtney would withhold her own judgment till she saw where this was going, if anywhere. She gazed at Lloyd's tight backside and became aroused again.

Wonder if he's up for another round?

A whole new woman had been unleashed inside Courtney, different from the shy, conservative woman she had been. She had no idea what this meant, but she intended to make the most of the situation.

"I understand," she heard Lloyd say into the phone before disconnecting.

"Is everything all right?"

He frowned, trying to ignore her sweet and slender nudity. "Something's come up. I have to go."

"To work?" Courtney blinked.

"Afraid so."

"Can you tell me why? Or is it top secret?"

"There's been a hit-and-run involving a pedestrian."

"Oh, no. That's awful." She winced at the thought of someone being hit by a vehicle.

"I'm sorry to have to run off…"

"I really should be going," she said, climbing out of his bed. "My cousin is probably worried to death about me." Courtney doubted this but it sounded good, anyway.

"I understand. Can I call you?"

"If you want," Courtney said as she began gathering her clothes that were strewn about haphazardly. The reality of her uncharacteristically bold actions was sinking in.

Suddenly feeling shy, she scribbled her number on a piece of paper and left it on the dresser. Whether he would actually call was anyone's guess. She certainly wasn't going to hold her breath waiting for him to.

Right now Courtney just wanted to get back to the comfort of her own house and warm bed. As well as contact Pilar to make sure she was all right.

Chapter 2

Lloyd was still thinking about his sexual tryst with Courtney and wondering if there would be a repeat performance as he pulled the department-issued blue sedan up to the dark corner of Boone Avenue and 85th Street—the location of the reported hit-and-run. The autumn drizzle made the road slick, a likely factor in any accident, but certainly not an acceptable reason for leaving the scene.

There were two police cars on the opposite side of the street. Ignoring its illegality, he made a U-turn, pulling behind one of the squad cars.

Lloyd flashed his ID to an officer. "Detective Vance," he said. "What happened?"

The officer's brow wrinkled. "Hit-and-run. Pedestrian versus a car."

"Is he or she going to be all right?"

"She," the officer clarified. "I don't know. To tell you the truth, from what I could see, the young woman looked in pretty bad shape. She's on her way to the hospital right now."

"Got a name?"

"Yeah. According to her driver's license, the name is Pilar Kendall.

Lloyd's mouth dropped. The name rang a bell. He knew her.

Pilar Kendall. They had gone out on a couple of dates, if you could call them that, but the chemistry just wasn't there.

He wondered if she was going to pull through and help them find the person who hit her.

Courtney tried Pilar on her cell phone and got her voice mail.

"Hey, it's me again. Where are you? Call me when you get this message. I had a very interesting night to say the least. I'll fill you in on the details later. Bye."

Driving her SUV, Courtney swung by Pilar's apartment on the way home. Knowing her cousin, it occurred to Courtney that she might have been entertaining a man herself and turned her phone off so she wouldn't be disturbed.

Courtney passed by an area that was cordoned off by

the police. Apparently an accident had occurred. She craned her head around, looking for Pilar's red Saab off the side of the road but didn't see it.

Thank God for that. Courtney turned into the Cherry-stone Apartments complex. She spotted Pilar's car in her usual parking space and breathed a sigh of relief. *Don't scare me like that, girl.*

So she was home. But was she alone?

Courtney decided to take her chances. Pilar owed her an explanation at the very least, plus she could share the details of her eventful night with Pilar in person.

She went up to her third floor apartment and rang the bell. Again.

No response.

Just as Courtney was beginning to grow impatient and head home, her cell phone rang. She was hoping it was Pilar. Better late than never.

Instead the caller was not identified.

"Hello…"

"I'm looking for a Courtney Hudson."

"Speaking."

"Hi. I'm calling from the Lake Barri Medical Center."

Courtney flinched. "What is it?"

"A woman named Pilar Kendall was involved in a car accident. She's in the hospital. Your name was in her wallet as a contact."

Courtney's heart practically stopped beating. "How bad is it?"

"I think you'll have to talk to the doctor treating her. I just wanted to let you know she's here."

"I'm on my way…"

Courtney resolved to keep it together till she knew the details of her cousin's condition, praying it wasn't too serious.

Courtney parked in the emergency room lot and ran across the wet pavement and through the double doors of the ER She saw a number of people in various stages of movement or lack of, including doctors, nurses and patients. She suddenly felt sick to her stomach.

Closing her eyes for a moment, Courtney took a deep breath. *Calm down. Pilar will be fine. She has to be.*

At the reception desk, Courtney tried to remain composed. "I'm here to see Pilar Kendall."

The receptionist looked up. "Are you a family member?"

"I'm her cousin."

"I'll tell the doctor. He'll be out to see you shortly."

As Courtney fidgeted, she spotted Lloyd talking to a nurse. What was he doing here? She remembered he said there was a hit-and-run. Surely they weren't there for the same incident?

Lloyd looked up when he saw Courtney approaching. She was the last person he expected to see again tonight. He turned away from the nurse.

"Courtney! Is something wrong?" Since they were

both in the emergency room waiting area, that was obviously the case.

"I'm here to see someone." Courtney looked at him suspiciously. "What happened with your hit-and-run?"

Lloyd lowered his eyes. "The victim was brought here. I don't know her exact condition yet, but I'm hoping I'll get to ask her some questions."

Courtney sighed. "Is the victim's name Pilar Kendall?"

"Yes. You *know* her?"

"Pilar's my cousin."

Lloyd stared with disbelief. "Pilar never told me she had a cousin." And one so attractive and desirable.

Courtney's eyes widened. "How do you know Pilar?"

"We met when I first moved here," he said awkwardly. "We went out a couple of times."

Putting aside the moment, Courtney felt a twinge of jealousy. Lloyd and Pilar? Had Pilar set her up with Lloyd, passing off Courtney a hand-me-down?

She glared. "Is that what you do—go from one woman to another?"

"It wasn't like that," Lloyd said, feeling defensive when he wanted to be above that.

"If I'd known you slept with my cousin, I would've passed."

"We didn't go there." Not through lack of trying on Pilar's part. In the end, she simply wasn't his type. "Besides, I didn't know you—or anything about you—at the time."

"Look, I don't have time for this right now," she

said tartly. "I just need to know that my cousin will
be all right."

"Ms. Hudson?"

Courtney looked up to see a man in a white coat
walking toward her.

"Yes," she said nervously.

"I'm Doctor Abrahamsen." He paused, and looked
from her to Lloyd and back again. "We did everything
we could to try and save her. I'm sorry—"

Courtney felt her knees grow weak and her heart
plummet, not quite ready to accept what she knew to be
true.

Lloyd walked into the police station the next day,
wishing last night had been just another routine night.
Instead he had to deal with the sad news that Pilar would
not recover from the injuries sustained after being hit
by a car. He felt terrible about it, especially given that
she and Courtney were cousins. He wasn't sure how this
might impact his relationship with Courtney. Right now
Lloyd was more focused on ensuring the hit-and-run
driver was brought into custody to answer for ending a
life prematurely.

After one knock on a half-closed door, Lloyd
stepped into the office of Lieutenant Steven McClure.
The thirty-seven-year-old single father was talking on
the phone—probably to his son, Damien—but raised a
hand to keep Lloyd from leaving.

Aside from being his boss, Steven was perhaps the one true friend Lloyd had made since moving to Lake Barri. It was Steven who had invited him to check out the Train Stop, then decided not to come in favor of catching up on paperwork.

Lloyd took a seat just as Steven hung up. "I promised Damien we'd play with balloons this weekend."

"You shouldn't make promises you can't keep," Lloyd said, raising an eyebrow.

"I know. Sorry about that. I really did mean to go to the club." Steven scratched his pate.

"No big deal. I did all right on my own." He thought about being with Courtney. "It's afterward that I ran into a problem."

Steven frowned. "Yeah, I heard the victim didn't make it."

Lloyd bristled. "She probably never even knew what or who hit her."

"We'll find out for her. The crime scene investigators have already combed the area and collected evidence."

"What evidence?"

"The usual—tire tracks, paint scrapings from the vehicle, victim's DNA, etcetera. It's just a matter of putting it all together to go after the hit-and-run driver."

Lloyd sat up. "The sooner, the better."

"As always."

"I want this case, Steven."

"I've already given it to Martinez."

"So reassign it to me."

Steven gazed across the desk at him. "Okay, what aren't you telling me?"

"I knew the victim—Pilar Kendall. We hung out a bit when I first got here."

"I see."

"No, you don't. I just happened to meet her cousin, Courtney, at the club last night. And we made a connection."

"Oh, and so now you feel obligated to make things right by finding this driver and making the arrest?"

"Something like that."

Steven leaned back in his chair. "Look, Vance, I understand where you're coming from, but that's not the way it works around here. We don't let the job become personal."

"It won't," Lloyd promised, though wondering how he could prevent that. "I need this one—if only for my own peace of mind."

Steven studied him. "Okay, you and Martinez work it together. But keep in mind I may need you elsewhere if something comes up. Remember this is Lake Barri, not Anchorage. Our force is stretched pretty thin."

"No problem. Whatever you need me to do."

So long as I can do my part to help solve this case and keep a connection with a very special woman.

Chapter 3

Less than twenty-four hours had passed since the shocking news that Pilar Kendall was the victim of a fatal hit-and-run. Lloyd was no stranger to people dying in his line of work. Or even personally, as his mother had drunk herself to death and his father might as well be dead.

But it hurt to see Pilar dead barely into her thirties. She was one of the first people Lloyd met when he came to Lake Barri. She was a fun girl, if not someone he could imagine falling for in a serious way. Moreover, she had turned out to be the cousin of Courtney, with whom Lloyd had an incredible time last night. Till tragedy struck.

He stood in front of Courtney's house. He'd driven

her home in the wee hours of the morning since she'd been in no condition to drive. The Georgian was two stories high with large bay windows and a red stone exterior. On a wide lawn were lilac bushes and a few Scotch pine trees.

Maybe I shouldn't be here. I'm sure she needs time to grieve. But I can give her a shoulder to lean on if she needs it.

Lloyd rang the bell and waited.

The door opened and Courtney stood there, backlit from inside as if she were an angel. He noted she was more casually dressed than her nightclub attire last night, but somehow looked just as sexy.

A slight puffiness under her eyes suggested to Lloyd that Courtney had cried a lot since he last saw her.

"Hello," he said in a low voice.

"Hi." Her voice sounded hollow.

Courtney was sure she looked awful but wouldn't apologize for it.

"I wanted to stop by and make sure you're all right."

Courtney couldn't help but look at Lloyd and think about their night of passion. But those thoughts were quickly replaced by her sorrow.

"My cousin is dead, so I'm not all right." With Pilar gone, Courtney felt as though part of her had been ripped away, much like when Joseph had passed away. "I'll be fine in time. Thanks for checking up on me."

Lloyd was humble. "It's the least I can do. I know you're hurting and probably have a lot on your mind regarding the funeral and questions about why this happened. Whatever I can do to help…"

Why is he being so nice and attentive? Yes, we had great sex, but he doesn't owe me anything.

Courtney sighed. After a moment she said, "Do you want to come in?"

He gave a slow nod. "Just for a little while."

Though Courtney lit a fire in him like he couldn't believe, Lloyd had no intention of taking advantage of the lady's weakness by attempting to seduce her. If anything was to come from their shared intimacy, it would have to be mutual and when a cloud wasn't hanging over their heads.

He followed her inside and was immediately impressed with the surroundings. It was spacious and open with plush carpeting and antique furnishings that had to be European.

"Can I get you something to drink?" Courtney asked as they stood in the living room. "I'm having cognac, but there's also wine."

Lloyd noted the half-empty glass beside a bottle of Courvoisier on the walnut coffee table. "Cognac sounds good."

"Make yourself at home," she said.

He watched as she walked away, then turned his gaze toward the brick fireplace. On the rustic wood mantel, Lloyd saw the framed picture of Courtney and Pilar. He moved closer. Though the two women looked nothing alike to him, he could make out some similarities suggesting to Lloyd that they were indeed cousins.

Courtney spied Lloyd checking out the photograph. She wondered if he was studying her or Pilar.

"Here's your cognac," Courtney said from behind him.

Lloyd faced her and envisioned their kisses that burned his lips. He took the glass. "Thanks."

She sat on the ginger-beige couch and he took the brown love seat.

Courtney favored Lloyd thoughtfully. "Do you have any information on the hit-and-run driver?" The last she'd heard, the person was still at large.

"Not yet," he replied reluctantly. "We do have leads we're working on."

Courtney stared intently at him. "You *will* find this person, won't you?"

"Count on it. Very few hit-and-run drivers get away with it." Lloyd tasted the drink. "Believe me, I want to see this case solved as quickly as possible."

You and me both. "How did it happen?"

Lloyd paused. "That's still being investigated, but it appears as though Pilar may have tried to cross the street when the car hit her."

Courtney's nostrils grew. "You're saying it was her fault?"

"Of course not," he said quickly, though she might have contributed to it by behaving recklessly. He hoped the evidence would prove that was not the case. "The driver fled the scene, possibly causing Pilar precious time away from medical attention that could've saved her life."

"Pilar didn't deserve to die like that." Courtney choked back the words.

"No, she didn't." Lloyd bit down on his lip. *I hope her death doesn't come between us.*

"We were supposed to be together last night. If we had been, maybe this would never have happened."

"Don't do this, Courtney." His head tilted. "You aren't to blame for what happened to Pilar any more than I am. You couldn't have prevented this. Only the driver could have."

Courtney dabbed at a tear. She conceded that there was no way she could have prevented what happened. Who was to say she might not have been the victim of a hit-and-run driver herself had the situation been reversed?

"Pilar always tried to live her life as though each day might be her last." Courtney's voice broke. "I just never thought that day would come so soon."

"I know."

Lloyd got up and sat beside Courtney. He felt as helpless as she did and wished there was more he could do to ease her pain, short of bringing the hit-and-run driver into custody.

Courtney was comforted by Lloyd's muscled arm around her. She breathed in his scent, remembering how intoxicating it had been last night. She tried to turn her mind off that and focus on the disbelief of losing her first cousin and best friend.

"Pilar never mentioned you by name." Courtney looked up at Lloyd.

He wasn't surprised, considering Pilar hadn't mentioned Courtney, either. "I guess we never got to know one another well enough to take that step."

Courtney took some solace in this, even though a part of her would gladly have wanted Pilar to be close to Lloyd if it meant she would still be alive.

"Pilar was always the life of the party," she commented.

Lloyd could believe that from what he remembered of her. "Does she have other family in Lake Barri?"

"Just me. Her parents died a while ago, and Pilar was an only child like me."

"Same here." Lloyd thought of how his father had just abandoned the family years ago, taking away all desire for his mother to have more children if someone else came along. As it was, she never married again, too disillusioned to do so. If it hadn't been for his great-aunt Mimi, Lloyd was sure his mother would have fallen apart completely.

"It was lonely growing up," Courtney said musingly.

"Tell me about it."

"I didn't actually get to know Pilar well till we were teenagers."

"I'm glad you were given at least some years to bond." *Maybe you and I will be able to do our own bonding over time.* His cell phone rang. Lloyd saw that it was work related. "Excuse me…."

He stood and Courtney watched over the rim of her glass while he talked. She imagined law enforcement to be a tough occupation and one in which a person had to have thick skin. Even so, Lloyd's actual body, while firm, was soft to the touch.

Lloyd snapped his phone shut. "I have to go. It's work."

Courtney frowned. "Wow, that's two nights in a row. Do you ever rest?"

He grinned. "There are times when they leave me alone."

She would have welcomed spending more time with him to share her feelings, but it would be selfish to think that his life should revolve around her. Particularly when they still didn't really know each other very well—apart from physically.

"You'd better go, then," she told him.

"I'd like to stay longer, but you're right," Lloyd said, handing her his card. "It has my home and work numbers, along with my cell phone. If you need to talk or whatever, give me a call—anytime."

"Anytime…?"

"Yeah." He smiled. "I don't want you to have to go through this alone."

"I won't. My friend Olivia is here in town, and my mother will be flying in, so…" Courtney paused. "But I appreciate the thought." More than he knew.

"It's good to know you've got a support group." *I'd still like to be part of it, too, and more, if you'll let me.* "I'll see you later."

Courtney warmed at the notion; even while having to deal with the very real sadness that came with losing a loved one unexpectedly.

Chapter 4

Courtney drove to pick up her mother at the Denver International Airport, forty-five miles from Lake Barri. The scenic route was normally a time to appreciate what nature had to offer. But, with Pilar's death, all Courtney could do was reflect on what might have been had the pendulum swung a little this way or that. She would miss her cousin more than words could say and could only pray that Pilar was at peace in a better world.

Something told Courtney that such peace would likely only come when the person who drove their car into Pilar was apprehended and put behind bars.

I know I'll rest easier when that day comes.

Lloyd had assured her it was only a matter of time

before an arrest was made. As far as she was concerned the arrest couldn't come soon enough.

Only then could Courtney get on with her own life. One that may or may not include the likes of Lloyd Vance.

Courtney spotted her mother rolling a suitcase toward her at a leisurely pace, seemingly oblivious to those whisking by in a big hurry to get somewhere. Dottie Hartford walked with a slight but noticeable limp, the result of a recent knee replacement.

Courtney met her at the baggage claim, longing for the days when she could meet her family at the gate.

Her mother had remarried five years ago after being a widow for more than two decades. Tiring of Colorado winters, she and her new husband had moved to sunny Boca Raton, Florida, shortly thereafter.

"Hey, Mom." They hugged, and tears welled up in Courtney's eyes. "I'm sorry you had to come under such awful circumstances."

But at least you're here. Pilar would be happy to know that.

During the drive home, Dottie pushed up her silver-rimmed glasses. "Lester wanted to come, but with his bad back and workload, we both thought it might be too much."

"I understand," Courtney told her, a trifle disappointed. As she had hardly gotten to know her stepfather, this might have been an opportunity to do that. Or was that being inconsiderate, even selfish? She couldn't honestly expect him to put his bad back at risk to come to Pilar's funeral. Could she?

Courtney took a breath, dismissing the thought. *It isn't about me, it's about Pilar. Let's not go there.*

"You really should get out more, Courtney," Dottie said bluntly. "You don't look like you're getting enough sun."

Courtney turned away from the wheel briefly and noted her mother's tan. "Funny, I was thinking that maybe you're getting a little *too* much sun these days."

"I was always a couple of shades darker than you, child. Living in Florida hasn't changed that any."

In Courtney's mind, their skin shade was once virtually the same. But why argue the point? "If you say so."

"What happened to all the lovely sycamore and cypress trees they used to have here?" her mother commented. "I seem to remember it being so much nicer this time of year with the fall colors."

"There are just as many trees here as the day you left." Courtney suspected she knew that but had perhaps become used to the swaying palm trees lining Boca Raton's streets. "And the colors haven't changed."

"Well, it doesn't seem like it to me."

"I'm sure it will all come back to you."

Dottie turned down the volume on the CD player. "It's so hard to believe Pilar is gone."

"I know." Courtney swallowed.

"She wasn't riding her bike, was she?"

"I told you she was hit as a pedestrian."

"And why wasn't she driving her car?"

"I don't know, Mom. Does it really matter at this point?"

Courtney bit down on her lower lip, trying to keep her frustration in check. No amount of second-guessing would change the brutal facts any.

"Just trying to make sense of it all. The thought that someone ran my niece down and just left her for dead…"

Courtney realized that her mother was hurting over losing Pilar just as much as she was. In some ways Pilar had been closer to her than Courtney, having looked upon Dottie as a second mother when her own had died. Courtney hadn't had such favorable treatment, however, often bearing the brunt of her mother's criticisms over the years.

"It makes no sense. These types of things never do. We can only try and remember Pilar as she was and pray for her."

"I'm sure her soul is already in heaven," Dottie said matter-of-factly. "What I'm praying for now is that the person who killed her does the right thing and comes forward."

"That would be honorable, under the circumstances." Courtney turned on her signal light. "But I wouldn't count on that. If the driver had wanted to do the right thing, he or she wouldn't have fled in the first place."

"It's never too late to see the error of one's ways, child. Even for something like this."

Courtney wished she could be as optimistic. Quite the contrary, she believed the driver was a big coward and would only come clean once identified and arrested. She was counting on Lloyd and his colleagues to make that happen.

The intimacy between her and Lloyd a couple of days ago entered Courtney's mind and she suddenly felt a burning desire to be with him. She fought off the overwhelming need, as this wasn't the time or place for that.

"So how long will you be staying?" she asked her mother, shifting her attention.

Dottie adjusted her glasses. "Till the day after the funeral. Lester can't stand for us to be apart very long. And, frankly, neither can I."

Courtney blinked. "I remember you and Dad being apart for weeks at a time." Her father's job as a development consultant often had him out of the country. "You once told me such a separation was actually good for a marriage. Have you changed your tune?"

Dottie sighed. "Things were different between your father and me. He had his job and I had you. That worked fine between us. With Lester we've become much more dependent on each other."

As much as Courtney may have wanted to resent that, the truth was her parents had the type of relationship that seemed to thrive on not smothering each other. Whereas in her own marriage, Courtney had rarely gone a day without seeing Joseph. So why shouldn't her mother enjoy the same type of relationship the second time around?

I only hope I get a second opportunity to find someone as worthy of my love and affection for the long term.

Lloyd Vance's image popped into Courtney's head.

After carrying Dottie's luggage to her room, Courtney made lunch and freshened up. Since Pilar's death, her colleagues at Lake Barri College—where she was a Social Science instructor—and a few friends had called or come by to pay their respects. For Courtney it was déjà vu from when Joseph died. Both incidents came right out of the blue and were hard to swallow.

She tried not to dwell on the sorrow, knowing Pilar wouldn't have wanted that any more than Joseph. Easier said than done. Once the funeral was over, maybe some semblance of normalcy could return to Courtney's life.

She served fresh carrots, brown rice, salmon and coffee in the dining room.

Just as Courtney had expected, it didn't take long for her mother to nitpick about everything she had or hadn't done to the house since Dottie's last visit. It seemed that the light French-gray color Courtney had chosen to repaint the walls last year was all wrong. As was the new plush carpeting she'd had installed. Even the ultra-expensive neoclassical furnishings that Courtney had painstakingly picked out had been trashed as being too bland.

"An old friend of mine is an interior designer," Dottie said. "Why don't you let me give her a call? It always helps to have second opinions, dear."

"If you like," Courtney responded, gritting her teeth. She doubted her mother would ever get around to making such a call, but definitely knew how to get under her skin.

And if by chance she did contact her friend, Courtney would politely decline an evaluation of what, to most people who came by, was an attractively furnished and acceptably remodeled interior.

The doorbell rang. Courtney considered this to be a well-timed interruption. "I better get that."

"Go ahead." Dottie patted down her blond bob in readiness.

Courtney expected that any number of people would be coming by, including those her mother had told she would be in town.

Opening the door, Courtney found Lloyd standing there. He wore a dark suit with a loose tie and was holding a paper bag.

"Hi," he said, a crooked grin on his lips. "Brought some doughnuts. Hope you like glazed?"

She couldn't help but crack a smile while warming at the same time in his presence. "Unfortunately I just had lunch. My mother's here."

"Oh, she made it. Well, I can check back with you later—"

"Who's at the door?" Courtney heard over her shoulder.

"It's just a friend." *Even if he came with certain benefits.*

"Well invite your friend in," Dottie insisted.

Courtney colored. "You heard her. Come say hello."

"Will do," Lloyd said.

Courtney took the bag. "I'll save these for later."

Dottie was seated in the living room when they walked in. Courtney wished the two did not have to meet for the first time under such circumstances. Or perhaps this was the only way they would've met.

"Lloyd, this is my mother, Dottie Hartford. Mom, Lloyd Vance."

"Nice to meet you," Lloyd said with a nod. He saw that Courtney was not exactly the spitting image of her mother, but the resemblance was definitely there.

"You, too." Dottie remained seated. "Pilar mentioned you."

He cocked a brow. "She did?"

"You're a police detective, right?"

"Sure am."

"Pilar said you two were dating."

Lloyd met Courtney's hard eyes. *Uh-oh*, he thought, *looks like Pilar's digging a hole for me even from the grave.*

"No, we went out once or twice but it was nothing more than that."

"I see," Dottie said peevishly.

And just what do you see? Lloyd wondered. *That Pilar exaggerated our connection for some reason?*

He gazed again at Courtney, only imagining what was swirling through her head right now. He knew he had to say something.

"Actually, I'm dating your daughter—"

"What...?" Courtney's voice snapped. She wouldn't

call what happened between them dating. Not to mention he still had some explaining to do where it concerned Pilar.

"We just started seeing each other. In fact, it was Pilar who made it possible."

Dottie looked up at Courtney. "You never mentioned any of this…"

"I never got around to it with everything else happening." She cast a wicked glance at Lloyd. "Besides, it looks like he managed to spill the beans for me." *Wonder how many other tricks he has up his sleeve?*

Lloyd could tell Courtney was pissed, but he would deal with that later. "Well, I'll leave you two alone."

"Yes, do that." Courtney wrinkled her nose. "I'll walk you to the door."

"We'll talk some more," he told her mother.

Dottie's eyes crinkled. "I hope so."

Courtney stepped out onto the porch after Lloyd. "Just what the hell was that all about?"

"You mean the dating part?"

"I mean everything."

"First of all, I told you I only went out with Pilar a couple of times. You know your cousin better than I did. I have no idea why she would say we were dating—unless she considered two outings in which we were never alone and strictly casual, dating. Maybe she wanted to impress your mother."

The more she thought about it, the more that seemed entirely possible to Courtney. Her cousin's usual taste in men—bad boys with little ambition in life—had rarely gained the approval of Dottie, who was like a mother to Pilar.

Even were that true, it didn't explain Lloyd's other statements.

"So when did we start dating and how did Pilar figure into that?"

Lloyd smiled at her. "I'd say we started dating the first time we hooked up. Pilar deserves some credit for that. Had she not gotten you to go to the club, you and I would never have met. Am I right?"

Courtney paused, finding his logic hard to argue with. "I suppose so, but—"

"No buts. Let's just leave it at that for now and see what happens, all right?"

"Fine."

Courtney wasn't entirely sure what she was agreeing to. Probably better that way. Otherwise she might start to believe they were beginning a real relationship, which scared as much as thrilled her.

Chapter 5

The funeral service was held on a Saturday afternoon. Mourners filled the rows of church pews, many drawn by the local press coverage given to the unfortunate hit-and-run victim. Dressed in black, Courtney sat in the front flanked by Lloyd and Dottie. Pilar lay before them in an open casket, looking as if she were merely asleep, perhaps expecting to be awakened by a kiss.

Courtney only wished this were true as she wept for her cousin. She glanced at Lloyd, who seemed genuinely moved as though Pilar really did mean something to him. Or perhaps it was more because he was still investigating the crime and seeing Pilar made it that much sadder.

For her part, Courtney took Lloyd at his word that

things never went very far between him and Pilar. Meaning that there was no reason why he and Courtney couldn't become involved, assuming they clicked as much out of bed as in.

The minister spoke with impassioned, heartfelt conviction. Though most of his words were about Pilar, her life, tragic death and soul, he also talked of forgiveness and prayer for the one who struck her down in such a horrific way.

While Courtney found it hard to forgive such a despicable act, she prayed the driver would do the right thing and come clean so they could all have some needed closure to this nightmare.

Courtney chose to say a few words to those who had come to pay their respects. She stood before them, fighting to hold back tears, but often failing as she spoke thoughtfully of Pilar's life, achievements, promise and how close they were. She would miss Pilar dearly and although the void left behind could never be filled, the memories would never, ever die.

"I'll see you in heaven," she closed with, and blew a kiss to Pilar.

Lloyd would have preferred not to say anything. He hated funerals. But after he thought it over, he figured a few words about Pilar might be appropriate, along with bringing people up to date on the case. At this stage, they hadn't gotten very far on naming a suspect. With any luck that would soon change.

"Pilar's death will not go unpunished," he promised. "Whoever did this won't be able to escape justice forever—not if I have anything to do with it."

It occurred to Lloyd as he looked over the mourners that the hit-and-run driver could actually be present. Hidden in plain view. Sometimes such a person sought to assuage their guilt by paying respects while staying at arm's length from apprehension. Could that be the case today?

If only I could read minds, it would make my job a hell of a lot easier.

Short of that, he could only go with the flow and let justice move at its own pace.

Just as Lloyd imagined his relationship with Courtney would. Having had his fair share of relationships that started off with a bang and ended with a dud, he couldn't begin to predict if they had what it took to make this one work. But since he was the person who had more or less shepherded Courtney into taking on something she may not have been totally comfortable with, it was up to him to at least meet her halfway.

Who knew how far they could go?

Pilar was laid to rest in the Rose Cemetery on a day that was sunny and bright, unlike the night that her life was taken away. Courtney said her final goodbyes, promising to always remember her, before inviting a few close friends over to the house, including Lloyd. Though their association had actually moved beyond the friendship stage, Courtney still had to get used to the idea of dating a cop—even one as sexy and hot as Lloyd. She was keeping an open mind after being on her own for the past three years, deciding to take it one day at a time for now.

Given the circumstances, everyone seemed to be spirited in accordance with Pilar's character and zest for life. Even Dottie was remarkably pert, surprising Courtney, who had expected the opposite.

Courtney was in the kitchen when her friend, Olivia Parker, approached her. The two had met when Courtney first started writing seriously and needed an illustrator. They had remained close through widowhood, divorce and professional ups and downs.

Olivia embraced her. "You'll be fine, girl."

"It'll take some time." Courtney blinked back tears. "Always does."

Pulling back, Courtney eyed the thirty-five-year-old, taller, slender woman with jet-black pixie braids. Less than a year ago Olivia had gone through a nasty divorce and had pretty much sworn off men. Courtney had also thought her days of romance had ended when Joseph died. Clearly she had been mistaken and felt there was hope for Olivia, too.

"We really have been through a lot together," Courtney said.

Olivia met her gaze. "And, God willing, we'll go through a lot more before it's over."

"I almost feel like Pilar's still here and this whole thing was nothing more than a bad dream."

Olivia held Courtney's hands steadily. "I know. Pilar's gone now, but I'm sure she's in good hands upstairs and counting on you to stay strong. I'll be here to help."

Courtney squeezed her hands. "Thanks. What would I do without you?"

"Apparently plenty, judging by the new man in your life."

Courtney blushed. She had introduced her to Lloyd at the funeral. "What can I tell you, other than it was an instant attraction?"

"I can see why. Both of you are hot to trot. The fact that he's an Alaskan hunk doesn't hurt one bit, so long as he knows when to thaw out."

"Girl, there are definitely no problems in that department."

"I thought not." Olivia grabbed a deviled egg from a platter. "And a police detective, too, who probably has a few tricks up his sleeve."

"That remains to be seen. Don't know if I'm made out for a relationship with someone on call 24/7."

"Who says you aren't? Give it some time and see how things go."

Courtney intended to follow that advice. After all, how could she really find fault with a man who was not only good in bed but investigating the hit-and-run?

Keeping up to date on how the case progressed was a fringe benefit Courtney embraced, especially on this of all days.

* * *

They rejoined the others and Courtney did her best to be cordial and not make it as depressing an event as she felt inside.

Lloyd saw that Courtney was putting on a good front in courageously making everyone feel at home. He was sure that Pilar would be proud of the effort on her behalf.

He followed Courtney outside for some air at her suggestion.

"Are you all right?" Lloyd studied the soft lines etching her forehead.

She sighed. "Yes. Just needed to step away for a moment."

"Good idea. I think they can survive without the host."

"But will the host survive without them?" Courtney half joked, already wondering what life would be like once her mother and friends had returned to their own lives with Pilar no longer around to lean on.

Lloyd put his arm around her. "Something tells me you will."

Courtney looked up at him. "So you think you know me that well?"

"I'm a cop. Instincts rarely fail me. Besides, now that we're dating, you'll have me around to keep from getting too lonely or just plain bored."

The notion agreed with her, as did the protective nature of his muscular arm.

"You sure you're up to the task?"

He grinned. "Yeah, I can handle it." Not that he would admit otherwise.

"We'll see about that." Courtney eased from his arms reluctantly. "Right now I'd better get back inside."

"Okay."

"Are you coming?"

"I should probably get going," Lloyd said, regretful. "I'm officially still on duty."

Courtney's mouth tightened. "Is this the way it's always going to be—here one moment, gone the next?"

He sighed, having been down this road before and not particularly liking it. "Not at all. But I am a cop and—"

"And duty calls—I get that. I just want to be assured I won't be the only one doing everything to make this work."

"You won't be," he promised. "I like you, Courtney. I also like my job, painful as it can be at times. Just let me see if I can find the person who ran Pilar down and go from there, all right?"

Courtney realized she was being overemotional and unfair. She surely didn't want Lloyd to compromise the investigation or his job by acquiescing to her every need.

"Don't mind me," she told him. "I'm just feeling sorry for myself. Do what you need to. I'll be here whenever."

Lloyd held her cheeks and kissed her softly, fighting thoughts that he was abandoning Courtney in her time of need. She was among family and friends, and he was still new to her inner circle. Whatever their future held would not happen overnight. He hoped they both had the staying power when the dust settled.

"Say goodbye to your mother for me."

"I will."

Courtney smiled softly, almost feeling as if he was the one about to hop on a plane. He gave an awkward wave while moving down the walkway. She waved back and headed indoors, relishing the quick but potent kiss he'd left her with.

Chapter 6

The following day, Courtney saw Dottie off at the airport and felt sad to see her leave. Though things had never been ideal between them, she never doubted her mother's love, even if it was tough love more often than not.

Her mother left with a favorable impression of Lloyd, which Courtney considered a stunning development, given Dottie's high standards when it came to someone being good enough for her daughter. Joseph had won her over, but only after Courtney and he had been married long enough for him to earn Dottie's respect. The fact that Lloyd had barely been in the picture and her mother initially thought he was dating Pilar made it all the more amazing.

Courtney refused to allow herself to get too carried away with Lloyd and their prospects just yet. Yes, she definitely was attracted to the man and the chemistry was there. But she was navigating new waters, at least since Joseph died, and felt it wise to tread gingerly.

Courtney decided to have lunch in Denver as she might have with Pilar, recognizing it was time to pick up the pieces and move on. Pilar would have been the first one to tell her that life was for the living and sulking wasn't part of the package. So why not listen to her?

Over the next week Courtney managed to clear out Pilar's apartment and office at the college. The process was painful since everything she touched reminded her of Pilar's life. Tearing it all down as though she'd never existed almost seemed inhumane, and at times Courtney found herself in tears.

In the end, though, it was all about the beginnings of closure. She donated much of Pilar's clothing and other belongings to various charities, aware that Pilar had done a lot of volunteer work over the past few years and would have been only too happy to give what she had to help others. Courtney kept photos, CDs and DVDs and some personal mementos for herself, as Pilar would have wanted.

Lloyd and Olivia pitched in to help when they could, for which Courtney was grateful. They were godsends that made the process much easier to deal with.

After their blazing night of passion, Courtney decided to slow things down a bit to cultivate a relationship with Lloyd. She wanted it to be more than merely physical if things were to move forward between them. Lloyd seemed to be of the same mind and didn't press for sex. Courtney's own willpower was being equally tested, since every time he was near her, she wanted to jump his bones.

Both would know when the time was right to go back down that path.

Lloyd thought about Courtney and wanted to kick himself for going along with the notion of getting to know each other while taking a step back in their relationship. It wasn't as if he was all about sex and nothing more. But after their no-holds-barred first night together, he missed exploring each other intimately and building on it. He wouldn't pressure Courtney into doing something she wasn't comfortable with. At the same time, he wouldn't stop wanting more from her if this was to work between them.

Maybe once the hit-and-run driver was apprehended— or sooner—they could kick things up a notch or two.

Lloyd was still contemplating that very possibility as he entered the office of Detective June Martinez. The thirty-year-old was several months pregnant. Her short black hair was tucked behind her ears, and she was stuffing papers in a file cabinet.

"Can I give you a hand?"

She turned her head. "All done for now."

He waited while she shuffled back to her desk. They

had been working together on the hit-and-run investigation, though Lloyd also had been preoccupied with a second case he'd been assigned to. Meaning he wasn't as on top of things as he wanted to be in finding the one responsible for Pilar's death.

"So how are we looking on—"

June cut him off. "I was just about to come see you. Have a seat."

Lloyd took a chair while she remained standing. "Maybe you should sit, too," he said, given her condition.

"I'm fine. So is the baby. She or he won't come till it's time, which won't be for a few months. Hopefully by then we'll have someone in custody."

Lloyd wondered briefly if he was father material. His own father was an asshole, but did that mean it had to run in the family? *I'd make a good dad at the end of the day.*

Why hadn't Courtney had children? Perhaps she'd wanted some but waited too long before her husband died. Of course, it could be that while she wrote children's books, Courtney wasn't interested in having any of her own and all the responsibility involved.

Lloyd refocused on the moment at hand. "Yeah, I would hope we'd have the hit-and-run driver long before that."

Small dimples formed on June's cheeks. "I was just joking, Vance. These types of cases generally solve themselves in no time flat. An arrest could come any day now."

Lloyd realized he had overreacted. Of course they would find the culprit in reasonably short order. The evidence pointed in that direction, even if a person of interest had yet to be identified. Or was he missing something?

"Were we able to get anything more from the tire tracks?" he asked.

June opened a folder. "Not much. The rain that night didn't help matters any, washing away potential evidence. We were able to ascertain from skid marks that the driver was going well over the speed limit. It's possible the victim misjudged that when she crossed the street."

Lloyd's brow furrowed at the image of Pilar being struck and the driver never stopping, as though she were unworthy of his or her time. "It's also very possible that she never knew what hit her."

"True. Either way, it should never have happened."

"Yeah, tell me about it."

"I do have something…" June removed a printout. "The lab analyzed blue paint scrapings and pieces of broken glass from a headlight found at or near the scene. Both have been identified as belonging to a current-year BMW. We're checking with the DMV to find out how many there are in the area, and hopefully we can get a bead on any that have had repairs done on the front end recently."

Lloyd nodded. "Good. We should be able to narrow down the owner of the BMW quickly."

"That's what I'm thinking. It's always possible the driver was just passing through. If so, it will take longer to ID them."

"My guess is the driver lives somewhere in the area, if not Lake Barri." Or so Lloyd tried to convince himself. "Given the time and place near the college, I'd say there's a good chance it was a student, faculty, or some other employee at the school."

"I'll look at their records for car permits issued and see if there's a match with the make and model of the car."

"Good idea." He adjusted in the chair. "I think we should also check out the local watering holes. More likely than not, the driver was under the influence. Someone might be able to identify him or her."

"I agree. We'll get the unsub one way or another."

Lloyd took some solace in those words, though the proof was in the pudding, as the cliché went. So long as the person remained at large there could be no letting up. If not for his sake, then for Courtney's.

Chapter 7

After a long day and night of working on her latest book and a restless sleep, Courtney woke with a start. It was Sunday morning, and waves of sunlight flashed through the scarf valence like bursts of energy. A loud humming noise made her wonder if she was still caught up somewhere between reality and dreaming. Then she realized it was a lawn mower.

Courtney got out of bed and peeked out the window. She saw Lloyd, bare-chested, mowing her lawn as if having not a care in the world.

I don't recall asking him to cut the grass. Or is this his way of working all those wonderful muscles?

She conceded the lawn had been neglected of late. It

used to be Joseph's job. Once he passed, Pilar often took it on, rotating with neighborhood kids seeking to earn a few quick bucks.

After throwing on a sweater and jeans, Courtney washed her face and padded down the stairs barefoot. She stepped onto the porch. Surprisingly, Lloyd didn't seem to notice her, so deep was his concentration. He was dripping with perspiration.

A flutter of fresh desire swept through Courtney at the thought of both of them working up a sweat in bed. She bit her tongue to hold off the notion, lest her will-power evaporate altogether.

She raised her voice over the hum of the lawn mower, "Good morning."

Lloyd turned, stared at her and bellowed back, "Morning, Courtney. Be with you in a minute."

He continued on as though he was mowing the lawn at his own house. She decided to go in and make breakfast. It was the least she could do for his trouble.

Ten minutes later there was a knock on the door. Courtney opened it and found Lloyd standing there, a towel draped across his broad shoulder.

"Hi," he said. "Sorry if I woke you with the ruckus."

"You didn't," she lied, and invited him in.

"I noticed the other day that your lawn was in need of a trim." Lloyd wiped his face dry with the towel. "I had some extra time on my hands and thought I'd swing by and take care of it. Hope that was okay?"

Though a part of her felt it was a bit presumptuous

on his part, Courtney could hardly find fault with the result.

"Yes, and thank you."

Thank you for looking so alluring this morning, even if you probably have no idea. "You're welcome."

"I've made some coffee, eggs and toast. Or—" she eyed his glistening chest "—if you'd like to take a shower first, be my guest."

"Thanks, but I'm good." Lloyd didn't want to impose, especially since he'd been hoping to get the job done and leave without disturbing her beauty sleep. But now that she was up and had invited him for breakfast, it probably wouldn't earn him any Brownie points if he smelled like someone who had just mowed the lawn. "On second thought, maybe I will freshen up."

Courtney smiled. "Good. There are extra towels in the bathroom. See you in a few."

Freshly showered, Lloyd joined Courtney in the breakfast nook. She welcomed his masculine presence but felt slightly ill-at-ease as a result. This was the first time since Joseph died that she had cooked for a man, albeit only breakfast. While Courtney didn't see this as betraying her late husband's memory, it was a turning point in her relationship with Lloyd that she accepted as a means for getting to know him.

But first things first.

"How's the investigation coming along?" she asked, holding a coffee mug.

"We're making progress," Lloyd told her without exaggerating just how much.

"Oh...?"

"We've identified the make and model of car and are trying to locate the vehicle and driver."

"That's good to hear." Courtney wouldn't get too excited till an actual arrest was made. "You would think someone would've come forward by now with information."

"It can still happen. Sometimes witnesses may not have even realized what they saw before, during or after the fact. Or they are too intimidated by the system to want to get involved. Either way, we'll get to the bottom of this, as is the case with most hit-and-runs."

That was somewhat reassuring to Courtney. She feared that somehow the investigation could get bogged down by other cases and might never be solved. Pilar deserved much better than that.

"I look forward to that day. My cousin should never have been the victim of some irresponsible driver."

"I couldn't agree more." Not to mention criminally negligent and quite possibly civilly liable for the pain they caused.

Lloyd took some scrambled eggs, wanting to change the subject to something that presumably wouldn't be upsetting to Courtney. Or himself, for that matter, as it was never very good to think too much about unsolved crimes when away from the job.

"So how's your writing coming along?"

That was a good question, even if Courtney suspected he was sidestepping the issue at hand for her own
good. She had been suffering from writer's block lately,
probably because her mind had been more on Pilar's
death than her book. Courtney felt herself slowly
coming around, thanks in part to Lloyd.

"Oh, it's progressing," she told him, biting into a
piece of toast. "Writing middle-grade children's books
can be an adventure. You never know where it will take
you once you get started."

"It must take some real talent to be able to write for
today's kids, many of whom have the attention span of
about five seconds at a time."

Courtney laughed. "I think you're right about that. I
suppose the key is simply keeping the stories interesting. It also helps to remember what it was like to have
an inquisitive mind and overactive imagination."

Lloyd sipped coffee. *Maybe this is a good time to
probe a bit further on the subject of children.* "Why
didn't you have any children? I mean, I see you as
someone who obviously has a gift relating to kids."

Courtney stared at the question, painful memories
flooding back. "My husband and I had planned to have
a family. We wanted to wait a few years till our careers
had become established and we had money in the bank."
She paused. "Then the accident happened...."

"Accident?"

"He was killed when scaffolding collapsed at a con-
struction site where he was working."

"Sorry about that." Lloyd reached out and touched her hand.

Courtney didn't pull away. "So am I. He probably never saw it coming." She thought about missing the opportunity to have children in her marriage. "At least I have my writing and lots of young surrogates to keep me busy."

But they can't take the place of your own flesh and blood. "That's true." Lloyd decided not to push her too much in this regard, as it was clearly a tender subject.

"And what about you?" She met his eyes, pulling her hand away.

"What about me?"

"Any children out there?"

He grinned. "Not that I know of."

"Then there could be…?"

"No children," he said succinctly. "Not to say that I wouldn't love to have kids under the right circumstances."

"Meaning finding the right woman who felt the same way?"

"Exactly."

Courtney gave a tiny smile, feeling warm inside. She could imagine him being a good father, just as Joseph would have been.

"So there weren't any women in Alaska to fit the part as a potential mom?"

Lloyd chuckled. "I'm sure there were some, but not the right one for me."

"But you had girlfriends?"

"My fair share. One in particular seemed like she might be Ms. Right, but turned out to be Ms. Wrong."

Courtney found it hard to imagine any woman not wanting to be with this man, who was not only eye candy but great in bed and not averse to being a father. Was Ms. Wrong the real reason why he left Alaska?

Maybe I should mind my own business. If he wants to go there, he will.

She moved on to what seemed like a safer subject. "Do your parents still live in Anchorage?"

Lloyd wiped the corner of his mouth with a napkin and looked down. "My mother died when I was ten."

Courtney cocked a brow. "I was eleven when my father died."

"Then we both know how hard that can be."

"Yes. You never get over losing a parent." Or even a favorite cousin. "And your dad?"

Lloyd frowned, though he knew that was coming. "He left my mother when I was just a kid. Never saw him again."

She was practically speechless. Abandonment and separation by death. No child should have to go through that.

"Do you think you might ever try to find your father?"

Lloyd stiffened at the mere suggestion. "Not likely. What's the point in reuniting with someone who made my childhood miserable and my mother cry or drink herself to sleep at night?"

"You're probably right." Courtney gazed at him thoughtfully. "On the other hand, after losing my own father, husband and now cousin, it's given me a greater appreciation for the value of family and the sanctity of life. Even a wayward parent might be better than not having any family at all."

Lloyd wasn't sure he concurred. A father who clearly didn't give a damn if his son was alive or dead was hardly worth pursuing. Assuming he was still alive after all these years.

"Blood is not always thicker than water, clichés aside," Lloyd said.

Courtney dabbed a napkin on her lips. Who was she to argue, never having walked in his shoes?

"Would you like more coffee, Lloyd?"

He was tempted to stay longer but resisted, knowing he'd much rather have her than coffee anytime. Courtney wasn't ready to go down that road again right now, and he had to respect that.

"Thanks, but I've got a few errands to run."

Courtney saw Lloyd to the door and thanked him again for mowing the lawn.

"Anytime."

"I may hold you to that."

She put her arms around Lloyd's solid waist, rose up on tiptoe and kissed him, unsure who pulled away from whom but loving each sweet moment their mouths were joined.

Chapter 8

Lloyd did some yard work at his house, a Spanish Colonial Revival near the lake. He had fallen in love with the place immediately. The architectural style was different from his home in Anchorage but still appealing, with smooth stucco walls, tall double-hung windows and a courtyard surrounded by Douglas firs. He got a good deal on the property and saw it as a keeper, unless something better came along.

Lloyd kept things fairly simple inside, not taking the time to do much more than put in some contemporary furnishings, exotic plants and a few abstract paintings. He believed the place was sorely in need of a woman's touch from top to bottom. Courtney came to mind.

Aside from liking the lady, he admired what she'd done with her own house.

He would be the first to admit that the thought of living with someone after being by himself for so many years was unnerving. It also excited Lloyd to think that any woman was enough to break through that fear and make him long for such companionship.

Courtney definitely had the right package, inside and out. But was she adequately over her late husband to truly want more from another man than a fling?

Only time would tell if they were both on the same wavelength at the end of the day.

Lloyd was just about to hop into the shower when his cell phone rang. He didn't catch it in time, but Courtney had left a message.

"Hi, it's Courtney. I wanted to thank you for this morning. It was nice getting you to open up a bit, not to mention putting on a show for me with your hard body. Good job with the lawn. Talk to you later."

He smiled, thinking the feelings of opening up were mutual. Only, her body was soft, supple, sexier and irresistible. He looked forward to exploring its expanse again and taking things that much further.

The next day Lloyd spent the morning finishing up paperwork from his last case involving an international fraud ring that extended from Anchorage to Honolulu, and had somehow found its way to Lake Barri, leaving one person dead and a number of others arrested. Later he would have to testify in court and hope the evidence was enough to secure convictions.

Lloyd took a call just before noon from June Martinez. She had been a no-show today and from what he understood, still planned to come in.

"Is everything all right?"

"Yes, if you mean pertaining to the investigation," June said. "But I'm not feeling up to par."

"Sorry to hear that."

"It comes with being pregnant. I'm not going to be able to come in today. I already cleared it with Steven. I just wanted to tell you directly."

"I appreciate that," Lloyd told her.

"I know we were going to go over to the college together and interview some people—"

"Don't worry about it. I can handle that on my own."

"I left the file on my desk."

"I'll get it."

"If you need anything just call me."

"I'm sure that won't be necessary. Just get well and I'll see you whenever you're up for it."

"I wish everyone at work was that understanding. Must be the Alaska man in you. I've heard people are pretty laid-back there."

"They are," he confirmed. "And they're pretty reliable, too."

Lloyd hung up and thought about the one person who had been anything but reliable back home: his father.

Maybe it's made me a better man having to grow up quickly and take care of myself. Maybe I have more to offer a woman than I thought. A woman like Courtney.

Lloyd entered the classroom at Lake Barri College where Pilar would have been teaching social science had it not been for the deadly hit-and-run. He headed toward the replacement instructor, Gail Ramada, as she lectured a group of students. She looked startled when he flashed his identification.

"Am I under arrest?" she quipped.

He grinned. "Actually I'm here as part of the investigation concerning Pilar Kendall's death."

"Oh." Her eyes grew wide. "I was so sorry to hear about Pilar. Whatever we can do to help…"

"I appreciate that."

A moment later Lloyd had the students' attention.

"My name is Lloyd Vance," he said in an even voice. "I'm a detective with the Lake Barri PD. I'm sure by now all of you know that Pilar Kendall was killed in a hit-and-run recently.

"Ms. Kendall was struck sometime shortly after teaching this class," he said. "We're looking into the possibility that the hit-and-run driver may have come from the campus that night."

"I thought she was killed near her apartment," said one student.

"She was, and it also happens to be close to the college. The direction from which the car was traveling suggests the driver may have been a student, professor or someone else associated with the school. We have reason to believe it was a blue BMW involved in the hit-and-run." Lloyd let that settle in for a moment as he looked around, wondering if Pilar's killer could actually be in this room. "Since many of you may have also left the campus grounds around the same time, I would ask you to search your memory for a BMW you may have seen driving erratically, or one you've seen since then with some damage to the front end. You may even know someone who owns one that fits the bill. You can reach me or Detective June Martinez at the police department."

That evening Lloyd brought Courtney some firewood, noting that the nights were beginning to get chillier and longer as fall began to wane. It didn't look as if she had used the fireplace in a while. If not, this was a good time to start.

He had begun piling up the logs in a corner of the porch when the door opened. Courtney stepped out, looking lovely as always.

"Lloyd…"

"Hi. Thought these might come in handy."

She smiled as much at the sight of him being helpful as imagining Lloyd being all bundled up in Anchorage and possibly even chopping his own wood.

"Thanks. In fact, I was planning to get some firewood soon. It's so much nicer this time of year when the fireplace comes to life, though I'm not sure it ever really heats the place up all that much." *Not like you manage to do all by yourself.*

Lloyd walked up to her, a couple of logs under each arm.

"I think we can do something about raising the temperature a few degrees," he couldn't resist saying.

"You think?" Courtney fluttered her lashes, remembering the last time he kissed her and not wanting to stop.

Lloyd wasn't sure if she was challenging him to prove it or just flirting while still wanting to stay away from the bedroom during their getting-to-know-each-other phase.

"One way to find out," he said, trying hard to keep his libido in check. "I'll just take these in and start a fire."

Ten minutes later Courtney was enjoying the crackling sound of the logs burning and a glass of white wine. She'd practically forgotten the days when she used to sit by the fire with Joseph. And maybe that was the way it was supposed to be when one person passed and another came to take his place.

Had Lloyd stepped into that role? Was he up to the challenge of a relationship with a widow?

"What are you thinking?" Lloyd stared into Courtney's eyes, trying to read her mind. He suspected she was assessing where they were now and might be in the future, just as he was. And she had every right to. Neither of them seemed particularly cut out for one-night stands, even if it had begun that way.

"The truth…?" She held his gaze.

"Yeah. I think I can handle it."

"I'm thinking that I really like you. And I haven't said that to anyone in a long time."

"The feeling is mutual."

Courtney focused on his mouth, wide and sexy with a slightly crooked grin. She felt her reserve slipping away, wanting nothing more than to kiss him.

And so much more.

"Stay here tonight."

He touched her hand. "You're sure?"

"Positive. Unless duty calls or—"

Lloyd had planned to update her on the investigation, but that could wait till later. "No duty calling me this night…"

"I was hoping you'd say that."

Courtney unbuckled Lloyd's belt, unfastened his pants and pulled them down. He was wearing turquoise briefs, which turned her on, but not as much as the bulge beneath that demanded her attention. She pulled out his erection, full and magnificent, and took him in her mouth. Basking in warm juices, she brought him to the base of her throat and enjoyed the immense pleasure he derived.

Lloyd ran his hands though her hair, looking down lustfully as Courtney orally stimulated him. He heard his own groan in the midst of her tongue teasing him up to the point of climaxing, and then retreating to prolong the experience.

When he couldn't stand it anymore, Lloyd held her shoulders squarely, squeezed his eyes shut and allowed Courtney to finish what she started.

Courtney felt Lloyd's thunderous shudder in the midst of his orgasmic release, and she licked him one final time, enjoying every sensation.

"You are incredible," he said huskily.

"That's what they all say," she kidded.

"And desirable as hell."

"Is that why your eyes are ballooning?"

"Yes, just as my taste buds are going crazy. I want you."

"I'm all yours."

Courtney was still amazed at how forward she had become in words and actions with this man. Even a pause in their intimacy had not slowed her heartbeat or need. She hoped he felt the same.

Lloyd placed Courtney on the carpet by the fireplace. The warmth from the fire heated his skin but was no match for the sparks that flew between them. He put his head under the crinkle skirt she wore, wanting to trap her natural scent within, stimulating his desire for her that much more.

With his teeth, Lloyd nudged aside her underwear and nibbled between Courtney's legs. She was wet and wonderful, imploring him through murmurs and body movement. He went to the base of the curly triangle of dark hair to her clitoris and licked, finding her even more appetizing than he'd imagined.

It was all Courtney could do to not scream out her

satisfaction. Instead she bit down on her lip, moaned and, when the moment of sheer delight came, squeezed her legs around his head, locking them in place till the orgasm had passed and she could breathe again.

She wasn't used to this type of intense satisfaction, but was quickly adapting.

When Lloyd came out for air, he knew they had only solved half their needs this night—saving the main course for last.

Courtney was thinking the same thing. "Maybe we should finish this upstairs."

"Maybe we should," he agreed heartily.

Chapter 9

"Got a second?" Steven stuck his head in Lloyd's office.

Lloyd stopped what he was doing. "Sure. What's up?"

"I managed to get my hands on three tickets for a Broncos game. Thought you might like to go with Damien and me."

"Count me in." He wasn't about to pass up a free ticket, even though he was more into pro basketball and eager to see what the Nuggets could do this season.

"Great." Steven sat down. "So where are we on the hit-and-run? I know with Martinez off and on these days, the ball's been pretty much in your court."

"That's true." Lloyd wished he could say an arrest was imminent. Truth was, the driver had proven to be more elusive than they had bargained for, thanks in part to some erroneous information. But his boss didn't want to hear that. "I'm getting there. Still got a few leads to look into."

"Care to share?"

Not really. "We think the driver drove a blue BMW and was probably coming from the college at the time of the accident. We're trying to narrow down local vehicles that fit the bill and have had some body work done. We're also looking for witnesses who can give us anything."

"Keep me posted. The sooner you wrap this one up, the better for everyone."

"Will do." Lloyd felt hopeful he and June would get the break they were looking for.

"So am I ever going to meet this mystery lady you hooked up with?"

A grin crossed Lloyd's lips. "Of course. Things have been crazy lately, but we'll all have to get together for dinner sometime soon."

"Sounds like a plan," Steven said.

After he'd left, Lloyd thought about spending last night at Courtney's. She'd let her guard down, just like the first time they were together, and had been fully into their lovemaking, as was he. He considered it another step in the right direction toward whatever the future had on tap for them. He intended to enjoy the ride along the way.

Courtney pulled into the parking lot of Red Sparrow's, an upscale restaurant in northeast Lake Barri. She'd agreed to meet Lloyd there since it was close to his house and she planned to drop by Olivia's afterward.

Not wanting to overdo it, Courtney had chosen to wear a simple printed V-neck dress along with a strand of pearls. As always, she kept the makeup to a minimum while scenting herself with a dash of Acqua di Gio.

When she walked into the restaurant, Courtney immediately spotted Lloyd. He was standing in a waiting area with his back to her, seemingly deep in thought. Suddenly he turned and broke into a smile.

"There you are."

She glanced at her watch. "Am I late?"

"Not at all. In fact, you're right on time." He kissed her lips softly. "And as tasty as ever."

Courtney felt aroused as she remembered their last lovemaking session and how they'd tasted each other and left nothing to the imagination.

"You look nice," she told him, admiring his suede blazer over a striped polo and dark slacks. She could smell the aftershave on his smooth, chiseled chin, the scent as appealing as the man himself.

"So do you. The word *beautiful* comes to mind."

Courtney blushed. "Thank you." No woman ever had a problem being called beautiful, especially when it came from someone so handsome.

"I believe our table is ready," he said, a glint in his eye. "Shall we go in?"

They sat in a corner booth and ordered cocktails while studying the dinner selections. Courtney had suggested the place, having gone there a few times with Joseph and once with her mother. She welcomed the opportunity to experience what amounted to a first real date with Lloyd. But hopefully it wouldn't be the last.

"What do you recommend?" asked Lloyd over his menu. Truthfully, he could eat just about anything. It was the company that made all the difference in the world.

"I like the teriyaki chicken breast," Courtney answered. "Along with some sautéed mushrooms and a baked potato with sour cream."

He nodded approvingly. "Sounds good to me. Let's order."

After the waitress left, Lloyd admired his date. *I could look at you all day and night and never get tired.* She had definitely put a spell on him, and he wouldn't have it any other way. And there was still plenty of time to add new chapters to their relationship.

"Pilar and I had talked about coming here," Courtney reflected sadly. "If only there had been more time…"

"Yeah, time is what we all want," Lloyd agreed. "Unfortunately, it's not promised to any of us."

Hard as it was, Courtney forced herself to turn away from such unsettling thoughts. She didn't want to make an issue of it, spoiling what was supposed to be a leisurely, relaxing dinner between lovers who were trying to build on that.

"I'm sorry," she said. "I don't mean to—"

"It's all right." He met her eyes. "We can't ignore what happened to Pilar and hope that will make it go away."

"True, but there's a time and place for everything. Tonight is all about us. Nothing depressing."

Lloyd nodded and lifted his glass. "To us."

Courtney followed suit, and they clicked glasses.

"So where do things stand in the search for the hit-and-run driver?" Courtney felt an underlying tension in the air while this case remained unsolved.

Lloyd paused, cutting into the chicken breast. He didn't want to paint too pretty a picture nor an overly bleak one.

"We're still trying to fit the pieces together," he said tonelessly.

"What exactly does that mean?" She was curious, as there was ambiguity written all over it.

"It means I'm not really supposed to talk about the case, least of all with my girlfriend, who happens to be the victim's cousin."

"I see." The sting of being shut out was softened somewhat by hearing Lloyd refer to her as his girlfriend. It didn't go without saying, even if they were dating and sexually active. But should their relationship mean that she couldn't be kept up to snuff on the investigation of her cousin's death?

Lloyd sensed that she was peeved and understood, though he was being put in a difficult situation. "You have my word that whenever something concrete surfaces you'll be the first to know outside the department."

Courtney accepted that, not wanting to overstep her bounds by applying too much pressure. "I'll be counting on that. I'd rather hear it from you than see it on TV or read about in the newspaper."

"You will," he promised. "But for tonight we're supposed to stay away from anything depressing, remember?"

"I remember," she said. "So what would you like to talk about?"

Lloyd pondered this. Were the setting different, he could think of a few interesting things they might whisper in each other's ear. But as they were at a public restaurant...

"What type of books are you into as a reader, Ms. Author?"

"I like the classics by such authors as James Baldwin, Ralph Ellison and Toni Morrison."

"I can see that. They've all certainly left their mark, as I'm sure you will."

Courtney raised a brow. "I doubt my children's books will ever put me in such company."

"I wouldn't be too sure about that," Lloyd said. "Some of the greatest writers have penned children's literature. Like Mark Twain, for example. Or Baldwin. And let's not forget J. K. Rowling."

"Good point." She couldn't help but grin. "Since when did you learn so much about children's lit?"

"Have to credit my mother for that. She put a book in my hand practically before I could walk and insisted I learn to appreciate the written word as she did."

"Sounds like your mother was a special lady."

"She was."

"Wish I'd gotten to meet her."

"So do I. She would've loved you." She certainly would have seen Courtney as good marriage material for her son. He would have agreed with her, even though such a prospect was a long ways off, if ever. No reason to jump the gun and spoil a good thing.

Courtney was flattered. Her own mother certainly believed him to be a good catch and hoped to see more of Lloyd.

I want that, too. Only time will tell if we can continue to click over and beyond the early stages of our relationship.

Chapter 10

Lloyd watched Courtney's car leave the parking lot. He would've liked nothing better than for her to come back to his place and let their carnal instincts take over. But that would be selfish. She had a life outside of him and vice versa.

There will be other times for us to play footsie in bed.

He drove home, watched some TV and called it a night—all the while thinking about Courtney, Pilar and how the two inadvertently came into his life, giving him more than food for thought on differing levels.

"Looking for me?" Lloyd asked June the next day, noting the expansion of her stomach. It never failed to amaze him how pregnancy seemed to give women a natural glow.

"Yeah. Got a lead on a dark-blue BMW that was seen at a tavern near the campus the night Pilar was struck. I think we should head over there right now. Might be a shortcut to identifying a suspect versus tracking down each and every BMW in the state."

"I agree." Lloyd turned an eye toward Steven.

"Go ahead," he said. "Maybe it will pan out."

"So how are you holding up, Vance?" June regarded him at the wheel.

Lloyd glanced her way. "I think I should be asking you the same thing, soon-to-be *Mother* Martinez."

She grinned. "I have my good and bad days. Lately they've been okay. Morning sickness can be a bitch and a half. But the joy comes in knowing my baby's just going through the motions till it's time to enter this world of ours."

"That's good to hear." Lloyd considered that Pilar had died before having children of her own and Courtney's husband had passed away before they could become parents. Was there any justice in the world? Maybe there would be some, once they nailed the hit-and-run driver.

"What types of crime were you up against in Anchorage?" June asked, regaining Lloyd's attention.

"Pretty much the same as here," he told her, not trying to be flippant. "We had our fair share of drug- and alcohol-related crimes, domestic violence and too much criminality involving youth than I was ever comfortable with."

"Yeah, that's a problem everywhere. Guess kids have too much time on their hands these days and don't put it to good use."

"I think you're right. Somewhere in there, though, the parents have to be held accountable for lack of discipline and the right value system."

"You're preaching to the choir. I'm going to do everything I can to make sure my kid doesn't end up on the wrong side of the fence."

Or even worse, the victim of a reckless driver, Lloyd thought. "So you think we might be on to something with this BMW?"

"Can't say for sure till we get more information. But my gut tells me the circumstances seem right."

Lloyd pulled into the tavern parking lot. "In that case, let's see if we can make some headway leading to an arrest."

Courtney walked into the lobby of the five-star hotel in Denver, where she was meeting with her agent, Sheri Geoffrey. She was in town for one day before heading back to Atlanta where Sheri ran her own agency.

Though having only met her in person once before, Courtney instantly recognized the tall, forty-something woman who wore her crimson hair in a flat twist. Sheri approached and Courtney grinned, vowing not to be as intimidated by the agent as in their initial encounter.

"Good to see you again," Sheri said after embracing Courtney and kissing her cheek.

"You, too."

"Glad we could meet on such short notice."

Courtney agreed, given that Sheri had only phoned yesterday for what was apparently an impromptu meeting. Since Lloyd and Olivia had other plans, Courtney had to go it alone to the Mile-High City.

They sat amidst a cluster of mango-colored chairs surrounding a rectangular glass table.

"I'm so sorry to hear about your cousin," remarked Sheri.

Courtney reacted appropriately. "It's still hard to believe Pilar is gone. She was such a fun person to be around."

"Did they ever catch the driver?"

"Not yet." Courtney frowned. "I've been assured the investigation is continuing and an arrest is likely to come anytime."

"That's good to know. Anyone who would do such a thing deserves to be put in jail, if not under it."

Courtney made a sound to indicate she concurred. Now if only Lloyd and his partner were able to make good on the promise of solving the case.

"On a brighter note," said Sheri, "I brought along the contracts for your next series."

A smile lit Courtney's face. Each new contract not only kept her writing career going full steam ahead, but was a stamp of approval from those who counted most: her fans.

* * *

The Cedar Club stood on a corner lot four blocks from Lake Barri College. Lloyd and June walked inside the dark, mostly empty tavern and made their way up to the bar. Behind it the bartender was putting glasses away.

"Can I help you?"

"Hope so." June flashed her badge. "Are you Clayton Newbury?"

"Yep, that's me."

"Detective Martinez, Lake Barri Police Department," she said. "This is Detective Vance."

Clayton hoisted a bushy brow. "You're here about the car, right?"

"That's right," Lloyd responded.

"It was definitely a dark-blue BMW."

"You're certain you saw it the evening of October third?"

"Yeah, I am. It was raining pretty much all day. I thought for a while, there, we'd have to turn this place into an ark."

"What time was it when you saw the BMW?"

"Oh, I'd say around 8:30 p.m., just before my shift began."

"Did you see the driver?" Lloyd asked anxiously, though this had apparently already been established.

"Yeah." Clayton nodded. "We both drove up at about the same time."

"Can you describe the person?" June narrowed her eyes.

"White male, probably late thirties, early forties, around six feet, and a bit on the chunky side with short gray hair."

"Are you sure about that? I mean, that's more than we usually get, especially since it was dark and, as you stated, had been raining most of the day."

"Just telling you what I saw. We were as close as you and I."

That was good enough for Lloyd, until proven otherwise. "Do you happen to know how many drinks the man had that night?"

"I know how many I served him when he first came in—three vodka martinis. Have no idea if he'd been drinking before then or after, since I had to go in the back to take inventory."

"Did he pay with a credit card?" Lloyd asked.

"Cash as I recall."

June leaned against the counter. "Anything else you can tell us about him?"

Clayton scratched his receding hairline thoughtfully. "Oh, yeah. He did happen to mention that he worked at the college. Since he was wearing a suit, I figured him to be a professor. But I could be wrong about that."

Or you could be right on the money. "Thanks for your help," Lloyd told him. "We may need to talk with you later."

"No problem. I'm here five nights a week and sometimes work the afternoon shift, too."

* * *

In the parking lot June gazed at Lloyd. "So, what do you think?"

He didn't mince words. "Given the timeline, the matching vehicle and a driver most likely under the influence, I'd say we need to talk to this man."

"I agree. And since we already have a list of school employees with BMWs, some who we still haven't been able to contact, it gives us a heads-up on who we might be looking for."

Lloyd's brow creased. "I just hope to hell a professor wasn't really behind the wheel of a car that killed someone who also taught at the college."

Instincts told him otherwise.

Chapter 11

The line was haphazard, stretching and twisting around two tables and an aisle like a snake. Most of those waiting patiently were women, along with their somewhat restless children. Courtney sat at the table near the front of the bookstore, a perpetual smile painted on her face. She graciously signed copies of latest book, *Melody Meets Her Match,* along with a limited number of her backlist.

Though her hand was already beginning to ache, Courtney shook it off as best as possible. After all, if these people could shell out good money to buy her hardcover book, the least she could do was autograph the title page and say a few words.

I'll never allow myself to get too big for my britches.

She was surprised to see the next person in line was a well-dressed man. He wasn't bad looking and offered her a genuine grin. Beside him was a pretty girl, maybe eight or nine, with a long ponytail.

"This is my daughter, April," he said. "She's one of your biggest fans."

"Hi, April."

She beamed. "I have all your books—except this one." April held out the book.

"Well, that's very impressive." Courtney took the copy and opened it. "What would you like me to say?"

The girl looked sheepishly toward her father and back. "To April, your best fan in the whole world."

Courtney chuckled. "How sweet." She signed the book and handed it to her. "Hope you enjoy this one as much as the others."

"I will," she promised.

"Thanks for signing," her father said. "She'll probably treasure it forever."

I doubt that. Girls grow up eventually and find new books and authors to fall in love with.

Courtney appreciated the thought nonetheless. "Bye, now." She gave a little wave to her fan.

For the next half hour Courtney kept up the pace, while doing her best to make every young reader feel special.

When the two books were set before her, without looking up Courtney routinely asked, "And who would you like me to sign this to?"

The amused, masculine voice responded, "How about signing the first copy to a very good Alaskan friend?"

Courtney raised her face to meet the gleaming eyes of Lloyd. She colored. "I never saw you…"

"That's because your attention was more tuned in to smaller fans. I promise not to hold it against you."

His lips curved into a smile and Courtney reciprocated, feeling warm inside.

"So what are you doing here? I thought you had to work?"

"I am on duty, sort of. My boss and friend, Steven, asked if I could swing by and pick up a signed copy for his ten-year-old son, once he knew I was cozy with the author."

"I'd be delighted to autograph it for him."

"The other book is for me," Lloyd said. "You never know when I might have a child of my own to give it to." *I hope that doesn't freak her out.*

Courtney's eyes widened. Was he being presumptuous? Or just tossing that out for a reaction?

Either way, the thought of having a child someday was one that captured her fancy. Particularly if someone such as Lloyd turned out to be the father, so long as that child was conceived in a loving and committed relationship.

She signed both books. "There you are."

"Thanks." Lloyd took them from her. "Well, I'll just go pay for these and catch you later." He wanted to hang around for a bit, but it looked like she had her hands full, and Lloyd didn't want to be a distraction.

Courtney said goodbye, wishing he could stay longer but understanding they both had work to do. Besides, they could spend quality time together later and maybe turn that into blazing passion. The mere possibility excited her.

She put the thought on hold and greeted her next fan with a radiant smile.

Two hours later Courtney was home and exhausted, feeling like she'd done her job well and made readers happy. She checked for phone messages. One was from Olivia, who had done a signing simultaneously at another bookstore in what provided them double coverage in promoting the book and maximizing sales.

"Had them eating right out of my hands," she bragged. "Hope yours went well, too."

Another message was from Courtney's mother.

"Hello, dear," Dottie said, her voice sounding as if she were coming down with a cold. "Hope the writing is coming along well these days. Give me a call. Oh, and say hello to Lloyd for me."

Courtney listened to the last message, then lifted the phone and pushed her mother's speed-dial number. She slid onto the couch and waited for her to pick up, wondering if anything was wrong.

Pretty sad when you think the worst whenever your mother calls. Maybe if we'd had a closer relationship there might be more reason for optimism.

"Hey there." Courtney spoke cheerfully.

"I see you got my message," her mother replied.

"Do you have a cold?"

"Wouldn't exactly call it that. More like a sore throat."

"Have you been to see the doctor?"

"It's not that bad," Dottie insisted and coughed.

"Well it never hurts to be on the safe side."

"If it doesn't clear up next week, I'll call Dr. Radler and make an appointment."

"Thank you." Courtney didn't want to sound like a nag, but thought it wise to err on the side of caution. "I just got back from doing a signing."

"How nice," her mother said.

Try telling that to my aching hand. "All in a day's work."

"Are you and Lloyd still seeing each other?"

"Yes. We're taking it nice and slow."

"Hopefully not so slow that you scare the poor man off. Since apparently things never got off the ground between him and Pilar, you shouldn't look too far ahead. You never know what could happen."

Courtney gritted her teeth. *Why does she do this to me?* "Lloyd and Pilar were never together—not seriously, anyway. As for him and me, neither of us wants to rush into anything. What happens will happen, regardless of our pace."

She saw no reason to mention that they were sleeping together while still getting to know each other.

"I'm sure you can run your own life without my two cents."

Thank you. "So was there something in particular

you wanted to talk about?" Or had they already covered the bases?

"Yes, as a matter of fact. Lester and I would like you to spend Thanksgiving with us."

"Really?" Courtney had never visited them for any of the major holidays, mainly because of a busy schedule and the fact she'd never been invited.

"With Pilar gone, I think it would be nice if we were together as a family this year."

It was still several weeks before Thanksgiving, but not much time to plan for a trip halfway across the country. There was also Lloyd to consider. She'd wanted to cook dinner for him. Or maybe he would cook for her.

"Do you need an answer now?"

"No, but let me know soon."

"I will."

Her mother paused. "You're welcome to bring Lloyd. I'm sure he and Lester would get along just fine."

Courtney pictured the two men in their lives coexisting in the same space. Could be interesting...

"I'll talk to Lloyd about it."

"Good."

"And don't forget to call the doctor if your sore throat doesn't ease up."

"I won't."

When Courtney hung up, she suddenly had some serious thinking to do. Would Lloyd agree to go to Florida for Thanksgiving weekend? Or could he not get out of work on such short notice?

Maybe he'd get the wrong idea if I invited him to spend time with my mother and stepfather, as if it implied more of a commitment than he was ready for.

Lloyd rang the doorbell. *Hope I'm not catching Courtney at a bad time. Can I help it if I love seeing her every chance I get?* He held the chilled bottle of white Zinfandel firmly.

The door opened and Courtney greeted him with a big smile. "Well, hello there, handsome."

"Hello back to you, beautiful and sexy lady," he couldn't resist saying, meaning every word. "I was hoping you were home from the mall by now." He'd even given her a couple of extra hours past the book signing, in case she went to eat or shop afterward.

"Yes, I've been home for a while." *And spent much of it thinking about you.*

They went inside, and she got a whiff of his fresh, woodsy cologne, invigorating her senses.

"I guess I don't have to ask how the signing went, since it's plainly obvious that your presence is in great demand by your fans."

"Yes, I feel very blessed. The plan is to keep putting out great material, and hopefully it will continue to pay off in dividends."

Lloyd grinned. "You're definitely a commodity I'd be happy to invest in."

Courtney smiled crookedly, realizing that she'd come across sounding like a stockbroker. Her eyes focused on the bottle of wine in his hand, barely noticing it before.

"And what's this?"

"Oh, a little something for us to share."

"How sweet of you." She took the bottle. "I could use a glass of wine."

"That makes two of us." He imagined tasting the wine from her lips, turning him on.

In the kitchen Courtney filled two glasses, passing one to Lloyd. She thought about her mother reaching out by inviting them to Boca Raton. Would Lloyd take the bait? Or swim as fast as he could in the opposite direction?

"How's the job?" she asked.

"Same old, same old." Lloyd tasted the wine. He assumed she was really seeking news on the investigation into Pilar's death. Instead he told her a bit about his latest case; but in the end, came back to the investigation that in many respects had brought them to this point. "We think we've got a bead on a possible suspect in the hit-and-run."

"Really…?" Courtney regarded him.

"Yeah."

"That's good to hear."

"Things don't always end up the way we expect," Lloyd cautioned. "We'll have to see how it pans out." The worst thing he could do was give her false hope only to find out they had targeted the wrong person.

Courtney understood he was trying to shield her from a letdown. But she was a big girl and had no illusion that every case achieved the desired results, even if Lloyd had promised such. She would be as patient as possible waiting it out till someone was not only taken into custody but actually tried and convicted of the crime.

They went into the living room and sat beside each other. Lloyd had his hand on Courtney's knee, which she enjoyed. In fact, every time he touched her, it was a warming experience. *This might be a good time to broach the subject.*

"What are you doing for Thanksgiving?" she asked casually.

Lloyd chewed on that one, assuming Courtney had beaten him to the punch with the dinner invite. "Nothing in particular. What did you have in mind?"

"Well, my mother invited us both to spend the holiday with her and my stepfather."

This caught Lloyd by surprise. He wasn't quite sure what to say before ending up with, "Wow."

"That a yes…?" Courtney batted her eyes.

"More like I'll have to think about it," he answered honestly. "Don't get me wrong, I'd love to visit your folks in Florida. But I'm in the middle of two investigations and still getting myself together in Lake Barri, so now might not be a good time." *Why did that have to sound much worse than I meant?*

"It's only for a couple of days." She slid away from his hand that now felt cold. *Is he trying to tell me something?* "Just seemed like a nice way to spend some quality time together." *Am I being too clingy?*

"I understand and agree." Lloyd felt her pulling away. "Let me check on some things and get back to you."

"Fine." Courtney wanted to slap herself for acting like a spoiled child. She hadn't even made a firm commitment to go to Florida herself, so how could she honestly expect Lloyd to agree at a moment's notice? Maybe she could make it up to him. "Would you like some more wine?"

He sensed she was coming back around. But Lloyd still wasn't sure if he was ready for a meet-the-parents type thing, especially when he had no one on his side to speak of.

"That sounds good," he said, holding out his glass.

Chapter 12

The Queen Anne–style Victorian house sat on a hill. A gray Lexus was parked in the driveway. There was no sign of the blue BMW registered to the homeowner, Gordon McNair, who taught History at Lake Barri College.

"You think McNair is driving the BMW right now?" June looked at Lloyd as they sat in a car in front of the house.

He eyed the closed garage and wondered if it was being used to store a hit-and-run vehicle. Gordon McNair fit the physical description and occupational status of the man seen at the tavern the night Pilar was struck. He also had a prior arrest for DUI, making him definitely a person of interest in her death.

"There's only one way to find out—"

They went up to the house and rang the bell. A deep voice inside yelled, "Will you get that?"

A freckle-faced boy of about eleven or twelve opened the door.

"Hi."

"Hello," June said. "Is Gordon McNair home?"

"Yeah. That's my dad. Who are you?"

Lloyd stepped forward. "We're detectives from the Lake Barri Police Department. We need to speak to your father."

The boy's eyes widened. "Just a minute…"

"At least he's here," June whispered to Lloyd.

"We can pat ourselves on the back once we hear what the man has to say." A quick confession would be nice; then the rest would sort itself out.

A forty-something man, dressed in jeans and a University of Colorado jersey, came to the door. "Can I help you?"

"Gordon McNair?" Lloyd met his eyes.

"Yeah. What's this about?"

Lloyd IDed them. "We're investigating a hit-and-run. Wonder if we might ask you a few questions?"

Gordon hesitated, looked back inside; then stepped out on the porch, closing the door. "What's this got to do with me?"

"Probably nothing," June told him. "Just trying to tie up some loose ends."

"So ask away."

"Could we go inside?"

"I'd rather not. My wife isn't feeling too well. I don't want to make things worse for no reason."

June exchanged glances with Lloyd. "We understand you're a teacher at Lake Barri College?"

"That's right. Been there for going on twenty years now."

Lloyd stared at him. *That won't earn you any merit points if you're guilty of leaving the scene of a fatal accident.*

"Do you drive a blue BMW?" he asked.

Gordon didn't flinch. "Yeah, so what?"

So it's time to get to the nitty-gritty and see if you bend. "On October third, a young woman was struck near the campus by someone driving a blue BMW. Witnesses place you not far away at the Cedar Club that same night, where two bartenders served you enough alcohol to put you well over the legal limit. And you left the tavern right around the time the hit-and-run occurred…"

Gordon sighed. "I was not involved in any hit-and-run," he snapped. "You've got the wrong person."

"But you don't deny being at the tavern that night?" Lloyd peered.

"To tell you the truth, I can't remember. I like to drop by for a drink after work two or three times a week. Last I knew that wasn't a crime."

"Maybe not, but leaving the scene of an accident is," June countered. "And apparently you like more than a single drink after work, don't you, Mr. McNair?"

His nostrils flared. "I wasn't drunk."

Lloyd's eyes narrowed. "We know about your DUI."

"That was five years ago."

"True, but—"

"Do I need a lawyer?"

You just might by the end of the day. "Not unless you have something to hide."

"I don't."

"Good. In that case, I'm sure you won't mind if we take a look at your BMW. Is it in the garage?"

"Yeah." Gordon looked Lloyd in the eye. "I'll be happy to show it to you."

Lloyd felt he was acting a bit too eagerly, while at the same time being overly defensive for an innocent man.

A couple of minutes later the detectives accompanied Gordon McNair into the two-car garage. The BMW was clean, as if he'd just washed it.

Lloyd inspected for any sign of obvious damage, particularly the front end. No broken headlights, dents or scratches. In fact, the car looked as if it had just come off the lot, which made him even more suspicious.

"Have you had any work done on this car lately?" he asked the suspect.

"Just an oil change," Gordon told him.

"Mind telling us where?"

"The local mechanic."

Lloyd tried to picture the vehicle ramming into Pilar, taking away whatever future she had. He wouldn't wish such a fate on anyone, even if it had brought him closer to Courtney.

"Does anyone else in your family use this car?" June asked.

"No. My wife has her own car. Kids are too young to drive."

"I see. Well, I think we've taken up enough of your time."

They walked out of the garage with him.

"We may have a follow-up question or two," Lloyd advised, adding for his benefit, "Strictly routine."

"No problem." Gordon closed the garage door. "You can usually find me here or at the college."

On the drive back to the station, June questioned the suspect's credibility. "McNair didn't seem like he was being totally straight with us."

"You got that feeling, too?" Lloyd turned her way.

"I think that he might be our hit-and-run driver."

"But too stupid to cut his losses when given the chance. We need to find out where that BMW was repaired."

"If I'm not mistaken, we've already checked off every local auto repair shop."

"So maybe it wasn't so local. Or maybe someone's helping him cover up the crime?"

"You think?"

"Wouldn't be the first time. McNair certainly wasn't interested in letting us talk to his wife. Maybe she knows something. Or there's something he doesn't want her to know. Why don't we get a warrant to take a harder look at this car?"

June nodded. "Good idea. If he's hiding something, we'll find it."

Lloyd got an adrenaline rush at the thought that they were closing in on Pilar's killer. Meaning he could soon focus more on Courtney and whether or not he was truly ready for a serious commitment when all was said and done.

Chapter 13

Two days later Courtney sat at Olivia's dining room table for a working lunch. Spread between ham sandwiches, salad and coffee were Olivia's illustrations for Courtney's next book, titled *Calvin and His Hip-Hop Friends*.

"These are wonderful!" marveled Courtney. "They illustrate just what I envisioned for Calvin and, shall we say, his rather colorful and loud friends." She grinned at the combination of human and animal characters Calvin had formed a bond with in his animated urban world.

Olivia sipped her coffee. "Glad you like them. I tried to make them just slightly eccentric with loads of bright colors, braids and big white teeth!"

Courtney laughed. "I'd say you accomplished your goal beautifully."

"No, I accomplished *our* goal." Olivia tapped her hand. "Which is to keep our editors happy and the young readers buying our books. I certainly couldn't do what I do without my favorite author staying on my behind pushing me to put forth my best efforts."

"Likewise." Courtney forked some lettuce, dripping with French dressing. "I think you know I'd be nowhere as a children's author without the world's greatest illustrator bringing my stories to life."

"Not sure I buy that, but it's nice to hear anyhow."

"It's the truth." Courtney supposed that if push came to shove, she could find a different illustrator or perhaps not use one at all and still be successful. Why mess up a good thing, though?

Olivia wrinkled her nose. "Some pair we are—two good-looking ladies with nothing better to do on a Thursday afternoon than look at children's book illustrations."

"Beats walking the dog, if I had one," quipped Courtney. Admittedly, outside of writing-related outings, socializing had never been her forte. Aside from Olivia, she had relatively few close friends who truly fit the bill now that Pilar was gone. When Joseph was alive, they would travel some and entertain or be entertained by friends, many of whom seemed to disappear after he died, as though she wasn't good enough to befriend alone.

Courtney was glad to have Lloyd in her life as a friend and lover, filling the void left by Joseph and Pilar. While she wanted nothing more than to spend as much time with Lloyd as possible, Courtney had no intention of crowding him or pressuring him into more than he wanted to give.

We're just dating, not married. I can't expect him to be at my beck and call.

"Jeremy invited me to go to Vegas with him next weekend," Olivia said.

Jeremy owned a sports apparel business in the city and had recently expanded to the Internet. Courtney was happy for her and sincerely hoped things worked out for them following Olivia's bitter divorce.

"I thought you hated gambling."

"Who said anything about gambling?" Olivia smiled sinfully. "If I wanted to do that, I'd stay home and bet on the Nuggets or Broncos. Honey, there's a whole 'nother world in Vegas these days. Or haven't you heard?"

"I've heard." Courtney put the mug to her lips. She couldn't help but think about inviting Lloyd to spend Thanksgiving in Florida. He had yet to get back to her on it. Was he getting cold feet? Or trying to find a polite way to decline?

Maybe he would be doing us both a favor by not going, since my mother can be quite a handful at times.

"Jeremy wants to stay at the Paris Las Vegas hotel." Olivia leaned on an elbow. "I can't wait to see their replica of the Eiffel Tower."

Courtney was envious, having never been to Vegas,

but tried not to let it show. *I'll get there one day. And maybe even to Alaska!*

"I'm sure you'll have a great time."

"Maybe you and Lloyd can tag along? Make it a couples' romantic getaway."

"Sounds like fun, but this trip is all about you and your man," Courtney said. "There'll be other times when we can try it. I hope so, anyway."

"I agree. I'd say Lloyd is the real deal and cares a lot for you."

"I know that."

"But...?" Olivia's brows drew together.

"Not buts," Courtney said. "Maybe just a touch of fear as to where this is headed and whether it's going to be on a slow or fast track."

"Which do you prefer?"

"One, the other...both." She laughed. "I don't know. I guess I'm still trying to get over widowhood and my skepticism about ever getting serious about someone again. Not saying I'm quite there yet, but I do feel good being with Lloyd."

"It shows. My advice is to let it happen naturally. And don't judge Lloyd by Joseph's standards but for what he brings to the table, which I'm sure is plenty."

Courtney couldn't deny that Lloyd was his own man and had enough to offer any woman. She took that to heart, wanting only to see this relationship prosper and be as much of what he wanted in a lady as she sought in a male companion.

* * *

Lloyd sat in his den listening to Sarah Vaughan's brilliant voice singing her trademark song, "Misty," a beer in hand. He was flipping through a photo album containing pictures of him and his parents. They were the only photographs Lloyd had of his father before he disappeared for good. He was a powerfully built man, and Lloyd bore a striking resemblance to him whether he liked it or not.

He'd thought his mother was the most beautiful woman in the world with long dark hair, smooth as silk. Till his father took that away.

Damn you, Dad, for ruining Momma's life and mine!

Lloyd turned the pages and got past his ire when viewing photos that didn't include his father. He wished his mother were still alive to enjoy life outside of Alaska, which she'd never left.

I could have shown you the world, if you'd only given me a chance.

His thoughts turned to Courtney and how lucky she was to still have her mother alive, even if they apparently didn't always see eye to eye. Better one parent she was in contact with than none at all.

Who knows, Dottie could even become my mother-in-law someday, if it's in the cards.

That would give him the mother figure he no longer had. And her husband could be a substitute father.

Lloyd put the beer bottle to his mouth. Was he really making marriage plans before any declarations of love had been uttered between him and Courtney?

Let's not get ahead of yourself here. We have a long way to go before exchanging rings.

He grabbed his cell phone off the table and called her.

"I was just thinking about you."

"Oh, really?" Courtney's voice brimmed with curiosity. "Is that good or bad?"

Lloyd grinned. "Always good."

"That's nice to know."

"I think I will be able to go with you to visit your folks for Thanksgiving."

"Wonderful."

"Sounds like a good excuse to get out of town for a few days and see part of the country I've never been to."

"I couldn't agree more, though I wouldn't count on seeing too much beyond Boca Raton," Courtney told him. "Knowing my mother, she probably wouldn't let you get very far."

Lloyd laughed. "Should I be worried that she'll pin me down?"

"Oh, no, not at all." Courtney chuckled. "But I just might."

"Hmm…that sounds inviting." He pictured her on top of him. "Maybe even a little kinky."

"If it's kinky you want, it's what you'll get." She swallowed abashedly. "Did I really just say that?"

"Afraid so, and there's no taking it back now." Lloyd took another swig of beer. He was getting aroused thinking about what kinky sex they could get into.

"You're insatiable!"

"I probably am," he conceded. "But only when there's someone who makes me that way."

"So, now it's my fault?"

He reacted with amusement. "Hey, there's enough blame to go around. I'm man enough to say that you really do it for me. I think the same is true for you as well."

"Pretty confident in yourself, aren't you, mister?"

"Would you have it any other way?"

She breathed into phone. "No, I wouldn't."

"Didn't think so."

"Things are starting to get pretty warm."

"We can make it *red* hot," he challenged. "Just say the word."

Courtney laughed seductively. "You want to do it over the phone?"

Not exactly what he had in mind but phone sex was a good start. And Lloyd was sure they would become so turned on that only a face-to-face encounter could set them free.

Chapter 14

"Hello, my name's Hugh Pesquera," the low-pitched voice said over the phone. "I'm your new publicist."

"You are?" This was news to Courtney, who was standing by the stove waiting for the teakettle to boil. Apart from her publisher's publicity department, she'd hired a Denver public relations firm to help establish an author brand that would translate into more sales. It had paid off, as her publicist—a hardworking, career-driven woman in own right—had worked wonders. So what happened to her?

"Yes. I'm afraid Justine Kerr retired and I've been given your account."

Courtney was shocked. "But Justine never said a word to me about—"

"It came as a surprise to everyone," he broke in. "But after thirty years in the business, she made a snap decision, or so they told me. But, hey, don't worry—you're still in good hands with this firm and me in particular."

Courtney was speechless. It had taken her a while to develop a comfort zone with Justine, who tended to be blunt in a tough love kind of way. Now she had to start from square one all over again.

Maybe I should just do my own PR work now, that I have a better handle on my career.

"I was wondering if we could meet for lunch this afternoon?" asked Hugh. "I can drive up to Lake Barri and be there by two."

Courtney mentally ran through what she had planned for today. *Guess I should see what he brings to the table.* "Two sounds fine."

"Great. Name the place and I'll be there."

She did just that as the kettle started to whistle.

Courtney used the time before their meeting to do some chores and work on her new book. After a period when nothing seemed to be working quite right with her plot, she suddenly found herself in sync with ideas coming left and right. Knock on wood. This would make her editor very happy, not to mention the fans. And even Courtney's new publicist, Hugh, would benefit, assuming she stayed with his firm.

On the way to the restaurant, Courtney thought about how the phone sex with Lloyd three nights ago had aroused her like never before when not face-to-face with an intimate. She had allowed herself to become totally caught up, something she couldn't have imagined before now. Though Joseph had been a good lover, he'd tended to be much more conservative than Lloyd, who had somehow managed to bring out the tigress in her.

Or was it more that she had brought out the naughty boy in him?

Either way, Courtney wouldn't complain. They were adults and had a right to enjoy each other's company, even over the phone.

At ten minutes to two, Courtney stepped inside the Aspen Grill restaurant, known for its simple but tasty lunches. She was told to look for a tall man in his late thirties wearing a gray felt hat.

That has to be him. The man spotted her almost as quickly, though the lobby area was fairly busy with people coming and going.

"Courtney," he blared.

"You must be Hugh?"

"At your service." He put out a hand, and they shook.

"Nice to meet you."

"Same here, though it seems like I've come to know you quite well after leafing through Justine's file."

"What on earth did she put in there?" Courtney half joked, imagining it held her entire history.

Hugh laughed. "Only the good stuff."

She smiled thinly. "Why don't we find a table?"

They sat by the window and had coffee while awaiting their orders.

"So let me ask you," Hugh began, "where do you see yourself careerwise, say, five years from now?"

Courtney contemplated the question. She had mainly looked at her career in terms of the here and now. Pilar's passing had told her that one couldn't afford to plan too far ahead.

"Obviously, I'd like to continue turning out bestsellers, make more money, and give back through conferences, conventions and signings. I've even thought about setting up a scholarship fund for aspiring children's book writers."

He grinned. "Good. I was hoping you'd say that. I'm the perfect person to help you achieve those lofty goals."

Like you'd say anything less. She eyed him. "I'm listening."

"Well, for starters, I think we need to work on your brand platform."

Courtney frowned. "Justine already did a great job with that."

"I agree. That said, I believe even more could be done to increase your visibility and, consequently, sales."

"Such as…?"

"Enhancing your presence on the Web with an improved blog, setting up virtual book tours and syndicated satellite tours and getting your book out to more prominent reviewers."

"That sounds good," she admitted uneasily. "And just how much is all this going to cost me?" Nothing in this world came for free and she didn't expect these additional services to come with the package she'd previously agreed upon with Justine.

"I promise you, not an arm and a leg," Hugh claimed. "I assure you the results will make it more than worth your while."

By the time lunch arrived, Courtney was sold on Hugh's new career strategy; pending discussion with her editor, agent and Olivia to make sure they were all on the same page. She understood that to make money you often had to spend it, but didn't want any missteps along the way if she could help it.

Courtney even planned to run it all by Lloyd. Though he knew little about the writing business, she found him to be quite knowledgeable about dollars and cents. She had also begun to feel more comfortable talking about her professional life and learning about his as they grew closer.

Lloyd successfully fixed a leaking pipe under his kitchen sink, then replaced a burned-out bulb before going outside. It was a chilly afternoon but nothing compared to what Alaskans were used to during the late fall and winter months. He couldn't exactly say he missed the worst of it. There were times, though, when Lloyd longed to return to the familiar confines of Alaska.

Then reality set in that there was really nothing there

for him anymore. His mother's spirit could follow him anywhere. And who knew where the hell his father was?

I don't need him to remind me how cruel life can be. He left us high and dry and there's no going back.

Wearing a maroon jogging suit, Lloyd started to run, making his way to the shoreline for a five-mile jaunt. He had only recently returned to the exercise, having neglected it while gaining his bearings in a new town.

No more excuses for not being in tip-top shape.

He hoped to coax Courtney into taking up running. Not to say she wasn't already terrific physically. But the sport was great for getting the heart rate up, working muscles and making you feel better from top to bottom.

He envisioned them with even more stamina while making love, arousing him. It could turn into a battle of the sexes to see who could keep up with whom.

His current cases flashed through Lloyd's mind. They were still working on connecting the puzzle pieces to tie their chief suspect to the hit-and-run.

Don't worry, Pilar, this won't end till the one responsible for your death pays the piper. Wish I'd gotten to know you better, but your cousin has more than made up for it. Courtney is a special lady and if things work out right, there's no telling where things might end up between us.

Lloyd was willing to keep all the cards on the table, even if there were no guarantees. He'd learned that from previous relationships that seemed promising only to fizzle out before too long. Maybe it would be different with Courtney.

His thoughts turned to the second investigation into the death of a teen runaway. At the moment, all signs pointed toward foul play. There were at least two solid suspects and more than one possible motive they were checking out.

Lloyd crossed the beach, noting the expensive lakefront cottages and flashy cars, before turning back around for the return home and cool down.

Chapter 15

Courtney left the Aspen Grill and drove down Pineview Road. She was still thinking about the meeting with her new publicist interspersed with Lloyd and the bridges they seemed to be building.

She was only a couple of blocks from his place. *Should I drop in on him unexpectedly? Uninvited?* Hadn't he done the same more than once? That was what people involved did and it was perfectly acceptable. Most of the time.

Opting to give him a heads-up, Courtney got out her cell phone and rang Lloyd.

"Hey, there."

"Hey," he said, sounding short of breath.

"I'm right around the corner and thought you might like some company."

"Yes, I could use some company—yours. I'm actually out running right now but on my way back home. I'll meet you there."

"I didn't know you were a runner."

"Haven't done much running since moving here." He took a breath. "But I'm trying to get back into it."

"Good for you." She pictured him working those quads and biceps. "See you in a few."

Courtney dropped the cell phone back in her purse. She imagined Lloyd would eventually try to get her to take up running. Good luck. Pilar had been a runner and she couldn't talk Courtney into it. She preferred to stay in shape through a combination of exercise bike and visits to the spa, along with long walks during the warm months.

But then, she'd never had a partner who was a jogger. Joseph was not much into physical fitness of any type.

Maybe I could learn to take up the sport with the right amount of persuasion. Or at least I can cheer Lloyd on.

Courtney parked her car in the driveway behind Lloyd's. She assumed he hadn't arrived yet. Gazing at the house that seemed way too big for one person, she pictured herself living with Lloyd. Wasn't that how most couples did it these days as sort of a test run to full-time companionship? Marriage?

Or was she reading all wrong into what they had?

Maybe Lloyd was happy the way things were right now—being involved while keeping separate residences.

Maybe that's best for me, too. Not sure how I'd feel if someone were living in my house 24/7 with Joseph's essence still there.

The fact that Lloyd was still single suggested he was not entirely comfortable sharing his space.

Courtney considered that her analysis could be way off base and more of a way to protect herself from being hurt.

Her reverie was snapped by a knock on the window. She turned and saw Lloyd's grinning, perspiring face. Courtney opened the door and got out.

"You weren't waiting too long, were you, to the point of dozing off?" he asked.

"I just got here," she said. "And, no, I didn't fall asleep. Just daydreaming." Good thing he wasn't a mind reader. One look at his glistening body really turned her on.

Lloyd was amused as he watched Courtney study him. He'd been surprised when she phoned asking if she could come over, making it only the second time she'd been there. He had begun to think she'd lost her nerve since the night of their first sexual encounter.

Whatever it took, he welcomed her back.

"Let's go inside…"

As with the first time she was there, Courtney was impressed with how immaculate things were: uncomplicated taupe leather furnishings that were attractively arranged. It was all the more amazing considering there wasn't a woman's steady influence. Perhaps she was still living in the past—her own past—when the woman handled the household chores and the man seemed almost incapable of such.

Did that suggest Lloyd was satisfied being self-sufficient in this respect?

"I love this place," she told him.

His eyes crinkled at the corners. "I'm pretty happy with it most of the time." *Especially when I can play host to a beautiful, sexy lady.*

"I think even my mother, the queen of criticism where it concerns the home, would be hard-pressed to find much fault, if any."

Lloyd laughed. "Guess I must be doing something right around here if I can win Dottie over."

"Oh, you managed to do that from the moment she thought you and Pilar were dating."

"But we weren't really," he reiterated, realizing this was still a tender spot with Courtney.

"I know that. The point I was trying to make is Mom thinks you're a great catch. If not for Pilar, then me."

He moved closer. "And what do you think?"

She took in his scent, a mixture of sweat and sheer masculinity. It was all she could do not to attack him on the spot.

"I agree," she said shamelessly. "You are a great catch."

"So are you."

"Then I guess we're both lucky."

"It's more than that," he pointed out. "We're blessed to have met and let things develop as they were meant to."

"You do have a way with words. Maybe you should have been a writer."

"Much better to be involved with one." Lloyd was close enough to kiss her and wanted to more than anything. But because he had just finished a good run and was hot and smelly, he wanted the lasting impression to be a favorable one. He stepped back. "Well, why don't you make yourself at home while I jump in the shower?"

"Thanks, I will."

Courtney watched him walk away with a confident strut, resisting the urge to follow. *You should have kissed him hard on the mouth and dared him to take you right here and now.*

She smiled at the devious thoughts he single-handedly managed to instill in her.

Oh, Lloyd, what on earth are you doing to me? Am I having the same effect on you?

Courtney went to the large picture window and admired the view. Colorado had some of the nicest scenery, with Lake Barri one of the crown jewels of the state as far as she was concerned. She was sure Alaska had its own breathtaking landscape and wanted to check it out for herself sooner or later.

She could hear the shower overhead. Thoughts flooded Courtney's head of Lloyd naked, water spraying over his hard body, her hands gliding the soap up and down sinuously.

Courtney's nipples tingled. She wanted him badly.

What's the man going to think if I join in the shower?
Courtney let impulses get the better of her as she began
unbuttoning her blouse. *Guess I'm about to find out.*

Lloyd stood in the steamy shower, eyes closed, mas-
saging shampoo into his hair. He rinsed it and contemplated his involvement with Courtney. The depth of it
sometimes scared him, having grown accustomed to relationships that inevitably failed. Could they dodge that
bullet and make this truly meaningful?

I'd say we're doing a pretty good job of it so far.

He felt a slight chill in the air and opened his eyes.
Courtney was standing at the opposite end of the tub
stark naked.

"Thought you could use some company...."

Lloyd had come to expect the unexpected when it
came to Courtney's boldness. He'd hoped she might
take the hint and go for it. He watched the water bounce
off her chest and stream down a flat stomach onto pubic
hair, totally capturing his attention.

"Oh, yes, I definitely could."

Courtney read the lustfulness in Lloyd's eyes, matching her own. She moved closer and grabbed the soap
from his hand, then began to play out her fantasy of
foaming Lloyd's body while watching his reaction.

Lloyd found himself unable to contain his erection,
which stood stiffly between them. That didn't stop him
from cupping Courtney's face and drawing their mouths
together for a long kiss. By the time they pulled apart,

he no longer gave a damn about the shower, wanting only to be inside her.

"Why don't we get out of here?" he suggested, the hot water cascading over them.

Courtney eyed him ravenously. "What's the hurry?"

Before he could utter a word, Lloyd watched with amazement as Courtney grabbed a condom she'd put on the tub's ledge. She sank to her knees, opened the packet with her teeth and put the condom on with her mouth.

Courtney rose and gazed up into Lloyd's eyes, letting him know that she was ready.

Bracing himself, Lloyd lifted Courtney at the waist and brought her down onto him.

She wrapped her legs around his back and gasped as Lloyd entered. While they made love he clutched her buttocks and kept his mouth locked with hers.

The old Courtney could never have imagined having sex in the shower. But this was a new age and she saw nothing wrong with letting her imagination run wild, especially when there was someone in her life whose fantasies seemed as sexually exciting as hers.

"Taking a shower has never been so much fun," Lloyd said in bed, where they ended up for a second round.

Courtney hummed and kissed his shoulder. "*Fun* is not exactly the word I'd use. *Erotic* is more like it."

"That, too." He grinned, a hand cupping one of her breasts. "Looks like we can't seem to get enough of each other these days."

"Got a problem with that?" She met his eyes daringly.

"None whatsoever."

"Didn't think so." She ran her hand along the side of his face, then got up, giving him a splendid view of the entire package.

"And just where do you think you're going?" Lloyd lifted to an elbow.

"You know, I didn't really plan this." Not in so many words.

"Who says you had to? Unplanned sex is always the best kind."

"Is that so?"

"Well, it certainly fit the bill this afternoon."

Courtney could definitely vouch for that, feeling as if all the stress had evaporated from her body. She began to gather her clothes off the floor.

"Well, I have to go now."

He got up and wrapped his arms around her waist from behind. "You sure about that?"

She closed her eyes when he kissed her earlobes and neck. "That feels so good. But I need to discuss marketing strategy with Olivia and my agent." *I had planned to talk about it with you, till something much more interesting came up.*

Lloyd was slightly irritated that she'd jumped his bones and was now ready to run off. Not to say that he didn't have a few things to do himself. Still, he would take an afternoon delight with her anytime.

"Can I at least make you a drink?"

Courtney wanted to pass, for fear that one thing might lead to another and the rest of her day might be shot. Lloyd was hard to resist, though, especially when those enchanting eyes bore down on her like that.

"Okay, but just one."

He smiled. "That's more like it. I'll meet you downstairs."

Courtney watched his enviable tight backside as Lloyd left the room without bothering to put on any clothes. She had a feeling he was hoping to tempt her into an encore.

Be careful what you wish for. You just might get it and have to perform all over again.

Something told her he was more than up for the task, making it all the more thrilling. She had met her match in the bedroom and so much more.

Courtney finished getting dressed and got her hair back in order before she joined her man for a drink.

Chapter 16

"The baby is kicking all the time now," June said, rubbing her bulging belly. "You want to feel it?"

Lloyd, who was sitting beside her in the coffee shop, was caught off guard with the question and unsure how to respond. He'd never felt a baby's movement in a woman's stomach. Not that many women, if any, had offered the opportunity.

He pictured Courtney as an expectant mother. She would no doubt be just as beautiful pregnant as not. Just as Lloyd's mother had been when carrying him. She'd taken pictures for him, hoping he could appreciate what it took to bring him into this world.

Lloyd hesitated just long enough to give June the wrong impression.

KIMANI
ROMANCE

An Important Message from the Publisher

Dear Reader,

Because you've chosen to read one of our fine novels, I'd like to say "thank you"! And, as a special way to say thank you, I'm offering to send you two more Kimani Romance novels and two surprise gifts — absolutely FREE! These books will keep it real with true-to-life African American characters that turn up the heat and sizzle with passion.

Please enjoy the free books and gifts with our compliments...

Linda Gill

Publisher, Kimani Press

Peel off Seal and
Place Inside...

PUBLISHER'S
FREE GIFT
SEAL
THANK YOU

THE EDITOR'S "THANK YOU" FREE GIFTS INCLUDE:

▶ Two NEW Kimani Romance™ Novels

▶ Two exciting surprise gifts

YES! I have placed my Editor's "thank you" Free Gifts seal in the space provided at right. Please send me 2 FREE books, and my 2 FREE Mystery Gifts. I understand that I am under no obligation to purchase anything further, as explained on the back of this card.

PLACE FREE GIFTS SEAL HERE

▶ DETACH AND MAIL CARD TODAY!

168 XDL ERR5   368 XDL ERSH

FIRST NAME	LAST NAME

ADDRESS

APT.#	CITY

STATE/PROV.	ZIP/POSTAL CODE

Thank You!

(K-ROM-08)

If offer card is missing write to: The Reader Service, 3010 Walden Ave., P.O. Box 1867, Buffalo, NY 14240-1867

BUSINESS REPLY MAIL
FIRST-CLASS MAIL   PERMIT NO. 717   BUFFALO, NY

POSTAGE WILL BE PAID BY ADDRESSEE

THE READER SERVICE
3010 WALDEN AVE
PO BOX 1867
BUFFALO NY 14240-9952

NO POSTAGE
NECESSARY
IF MAILED
IN THE
UNITED STATES

"Come on, Vance, don't be shy. He won't bite you—not yet. I promise."

Lloyd grinned. "You had me worried for a minute there." He reached out and gently put his hand on her stomach.

June laughed. "You'll have to press a bit harder than that. I'm not so fragile, even if I may look that way."

He moved his hand around the blouse covering her stomach more firmly. "When did you learn it was a boy?"

"Last week. My husband decided he couldn't wait any longer to find out. I think he was a little relieved, to tell you the truth. This way he can teach him all the tricks of becoming a man."

"I can feel him kicking," Lloyd declared, almost as if he was a proud papa himself. "Amazing."

"Yes, it is." June met his eyes with amusement. "I'm sure it was just as amazing for pregnant women you knew in Alaska."

"Of course." He removed his hand. "Your husband's a lucky man."

"I think I'm pretty lucky, too. It took two to create this masterpiece."

"You're both very fortunate, June. My hat's off to you." Lloyd tipped an imaginary hat.

"If Ricardo has his way, we'll be blessed with several more little ones. I'm not so sure about that. Career versus motherhood can be a real balancing act."

"I think I understand where you're coming from." He imagined Courtney faced the same dilemma in her marriage before fate stepped in. But what about now? Would her career come first over family?

Lloyd asked himself the same question. *I'd never put law enforcement over my wife and kids.* He conceded that he'd never been put to the test thus far. Would that make a difference?

"So how are things with you and your girlfriend?" June gazed at him over a mug of steaming chai tea.

Lloyd had shared a few tidbits about their relationship, since Courtney was Pilar's cousin. "Great. No complaints."

She cracked a smile. "Sounds like you're still in the honeymoon stage where neither of you can do any wrong. Enjoy it while you can."

He chuckled. "Seems to me you're still on an extended honeymoon yourself and ready to build on that."

"I suppose I am at that. Good one, Vance."

"Hey, just telling it like it is."

Lloyd finished his coffee. *Maybe it takes getting hitched for the claws to come out in a relationship.* He discounted that theory, considering some of his previous relationships had been tumultuous practically from start to finish. He may have found his true soul mate in Courtney.

"Let's get out of here and pay our auto repair shop a little visit," June said.

Lloyd agreed, hoping they had pinpointed the right place this time that could help tie the pieces together in their hunt for a hit-and-run driver.

* * *

Courtney was in the living room working on her laptop, listening to Mozart. Classical music always relaxed her and she preferred it to anything else when she focused on rewrites. She took a moment to recall her impromptu visit to Lloyd's house the day before last. It hadn't taken long for desires to turn into all-consuming passions that had left both of them breathless more than once.

I just can't believe I actually seduced the man right there in his shower. Not that I heard one word of complaint.

She felt a prickle between her legs and Courtney allowed her mind to wander a bit further before getting back to the project at hand. Lloyd Vance was definitely reeling her in like a salmon and there seemed to be nothing she could do other than be held captive by him hook, line and sinker.

Wherever this journey was leading, Courtney was ready for the ride, though not sure what the emotional toll would be for a widow ready for love and marriage again. But she would allow Lloyd to move at his own pace.

Courtney had gone through a few pages of manuscript when the doorbell rang. She thought it might be Lloyd stopping by for a repeat performance, but instead found an attractive woman at her door.

"Hi. Are you Courtney?"

"Yes."

"My name's Gail Ramada. I'm teaching Pilar's classes at the college."

"Hi." Courtney met her eyes.

"Pilar left behind a few things, and I thought you might like to have them."

"Oh. Would you like to come in?"

"Sure, for a few minutes."

Courtney welcomed the opportunity to reconnect with her late cousin, even through a stranger.

"I didn't know Pilar very well, but we talked every now and then." Gail glanced about. "She told me about her cousin the famous writer."

Courtney blushed. "I don't know if I'd call myself famous, but writing is my vocation."

"Well, I applaud you for that. For me, grading papers can be too much sometimes."

"Pilar used to say the same thing. I admire anyone able to teach others to find their way in life."

"I do teach them. They don't always listen." Gail handed Courtney a bag. "It has some of Pilar's papers, a few CDs and a picture she kept of the two of you."

Courtney opened the bag and removed the five-by-seven, framed photograph. It was taken a year and a half ago at the cabin they owned in the mountains. The thought that it was the last picture of them together made Courtney want to cry.

"Thanks for bringing her things," she told Gail, forcing a smile. "I think about Pilar every day and miss her a lot."

"I can understand that. I lost a brother a few years ago, and I'm still trying to come to terms with it."

Courtney looked at her sadly. "How did he die?"

"An aneurysm."

"I'm sorry about that."

"He went quickly." Gail sighed and changed the subject. "I hear the police still haven't arrested anyone for Pilar's death…"

Courtney winced at the reality. Lloyd had indicated that it was practically a mere formality at this point. But the proof was in the pudding. Until it actually happened, someone was out there free as a bird while Pilar lay in a casket, her life snuffed out like a candle before its time.

Courtney glanced at her houseguest and Pilar's former colleague. "Would you like some coffee or tea?"

Lloyd pulled inside the small parking lot of Raphael's Auto Repair. He unbuckled his seat belt and glanced at June and then the warrant they had obtained to inspect Gordon McNair's vehicle. "This place can't be more than a mile from Gordon McNair's house. If his car was used in the hit-and-run, it damn sure didn't repair itself."

"Maybe the mechanic who was on duty at the time can shed some light on the issue." she said, scratching an eyebrow.

"Yeah, that would be nice."

A minute later they were inside a small lobby and went up to a counter.

"Can I help you?" the woman at the counter asked.

"We're detectives from the police department," June

responded, flashing her badge. "We'd like to see Raphael—"

The woman called out to the garage. Within moments a tall, wiry man in his fifties emerged wearing an oil-stained uniform.

"Raphael Newberg?" Lloyd asked.

"Yeah. What can I do you for?"

"We're investigating a hit-and-run and we believe the driver may have had some work done on his BMW here."

Raphael nodded. "Yeah, I believe we spoke on the phone. I think I can help you."

Lloyd and June accompanied him to a back office, where they were shown the records of car repairs over a two-week stretch in early October.

"We worked on a BMW October fifth," Raphael said. "It had a busted headlight, some damage to the front end and lots of scratches on the paint job."

June studied the repair order. "It says the payment was made in cash."

"That's right. The driver insisted upon it."

Looking over her shoulder, Lloyd noted that the driver's signature was illegible. But the license plate number was clear and a perfect match for that registered to Gordon McNair's BMW.

"Why wasn't this reported to the authorities?" Lloyd gazed at the mechanic.

"We had no way of knowing the car was involved in a hit-and-run. As I recall, the driver claimed he'd hit a deer."

Lloyd wanted to be pissed, especially since this misinformation had stalled an investigation that he wanted over as much for Courtney as himself. But apparently it was pretty common around there to hit a deer crossing the road. Probably something McNair was counting on to evade the law and dupe the repair shop.

"You may be called upon to testify in court," Lloyd warned.

Raphael shrugged. "Hey, anything I can do to help."

You've already helped in a big way. McNair has backed himself into a corner that he won't be able to worm his way out of.

"We'll be in touch."

It didn't take long for a warrant to be issued for the arrest of Gordon McNair. Though the case was still largely circumstantial, the pieces fit. Lloyd was convinced that they had their hit-and-run driver. June concurred and Steven signed off on the paperwork.

Lloyd would've preferred to arrest McNair right away, which meant taking him into custody at his house. But June balked at that, not wanting to make the arrest in front of his family. As a soon-to-be parent, she was concerned about the effect it might have on McNair's two children. Lloyd acquiesced, understanding firsthand how a traumatic event could scar a child forever.

They waited till the following day for McNair to arrive at college, allowing him to pull the BMW into his regular parking place before approaching.

"Think he'll try anything stupid?" Lloyd asked June.

"Not likely. Hit-and-run drivers don't usually want to kill themselves or try to make a run for it when there's nowhere to go."

"Yeah, they usually prefer to run and hide, hoping it will all just go away. Fat chance."

The suspect emerged from his car, seemingly caught up in his own world—one that didn't include being taken into custody.

"Gordon McNair," voiced Lloyd, backed by June and gun-wielding officers, "you're under arrest for the hit-and-run death of Pilar Kendall. Put your hands up—"

He looked stunned. "You're making a big mistake!"

Lloyd slapped the handcuffs on him confidently. "No, *you* made one when you decided not to stop after your car plowed into someone."

The two were eyeball to eyeball before the suspect turned away, apparently reconciled to his fate. Lloyd saw this as the beginning of the end of this case, barring any unforeseen circumstances.

"Take him away," he ordered.

Chapter 17

Lloyd phoned Courtney with the news before she could see it on TV. "We got him."

"Really…?" Courtney caught her breath.

"Yeah, the man who took Pilar away is now behind bars. And he's talking—"

Anger took hold of her. "So what is he saying? I suppose he's trying to justify the unjustifiable with some lame excuse?"

"Same old, same old," Lloyd stated. "Claims he never even saw Pilar till the last moment. Then he panicked and took off."

"And that's supposed to make it all right?"

"Not in my book. We can't bring your cousin back, but at least this guy will have to answer for what he did."

"I'm glad for that." Courtney's eyes watered. "Thank you for not giving up on this."

"Not a chance. I owed it to Pilar to see that justice was served."

"I'm sure she's more at peace now."

"I hope so." He paused. "I think Pilar would have been happy for us at the end of the day."

Would she? Courtney wasn't sure about that. Not when her cousin liked Lloyd enough to exaggerate their relationship, though, oddly, Pilar hadn't seen fit to mention Lloyd by name to Courtney. Might that have made a difference in the scheme of things? Or had she been destined to get involved with Lloyd no matter what?

"Maybe she would have," Courtney said, thankful they never had to go down that road. The last thing she would have wanted was for a man to come between her and Pilar. Especially one as wonderful as Lloyd. Courtney could envision them fighting over him tooth and nail. "Would you like to come over?"

Lloyd hesitated. "Actually, I thought I'd go for a drink with some of the people from work to celebrate the arrest. I can swing by your place afterward, though, if you like."

"No, that's all right." It would be selfish of her to want to hog his time, so Courtney didn't make waves. "Go ahead and have fun with your colleagues."

"You're sure?"

"Of course. You've earned it for a job well done. We can see each other tomorrow."

"Okay." He made a kissing noise.

She did the same and hung up before letting her tears flow for Pilar. *I know you heard that from up there, cuz. The bastard who sent you to heaven much too soon has been apprehended. You can rest now. I'll be talking to you.*

Courtney wiped her eyes and was about to head downstairs when the phone rang again. This time it was Olivia.

"Did you hear the news?"

"Lloyd just told me," Courtney replied.

"You must be so relieved to know the jerk was caught."

"I am. But that still won't bring Pilar back."

"I know, but at least her death won't go unanswered."

"You're right." Courtney would not allow the hit-and-run driver to deprive her of that victory, even if Pilar wasn't there to share the moment.

"I say we go out and celebrate," Olivia said.

"I don't know—"

"Oh, come on, girl. You deserve this and we both know Pilar would be the first one to drag you to a club if she were still here."

Courtney smiled and pictured her cousin doing that very thing. *Guess I need to lighten up and rejoice that Lloyd and company came through for me and Pilar.*

"Okay, you talked me into it. Where do you want to go?"

"Let's check out the Train Stop. I hear they really know how to party there!"

* * *

"So this is where all the action takes place," commented Steven, sitting at a table beside Lloyd and June in the crowded Train Stop.

"I wouldn't know," June said, sipping a Shirley Temple. "I've got all the action I need at home, with an addition on the way. Vance here, on the other hand, with no such responsibilities, is probably still sowing his oats."

"That's not what I hear. He's found a lady to keep him on a leash."

Lloyd laughed uneasily while shouldering the playful barbs. Could he help it if circumstances had prevented him from becoming a father so far? "I'm not anyone's dog and way past sowing oats," he said over a brandy Alexander. "But I am involved with a wonderful woman."

"Big difference between being involved and having a ring on your finger," June told him. "In the latter instance, there's always someone to answer to whether you like or not."

"It's called choice," he responded. "What works for one doesn't necessarily for another."

"Point taken. For your sake, I hope you make the choice that does work, assuming you haven't already."

Lloyd sat back. "Things are pretty good for us right now. That's all I can ask."

"Can't hurt your cause any to have made an arrest in the hit-and-run," Steven said. "Courtney won't be able to somehow hold that against you, were that the case."

"It wasn't," he insisted, though Lloyd admittedly felt as if a huge burden had been removed from his shoulders in the growth of their relationship. "She wanted someone held accountable for her cousin's death as much as anyone, and I can't blame her one bit for that."

"Neither can I."

June looked at Lloyd. "So what do you suppose will happen with McNair now that he's in custody?"

He shrugged. "Chances are he'll just end up copping a plea. Since McNair's already confessed, seems that's the way it usually works in the best interests of all concerned." Including Courtney, who, Lloyd was sure, would want this over with as soon as possible without having to rehash the horrible details in a trial.

"I'm sure you're right, till the next drunk driver cuts down someone else and flees the scene."

"Yeah." Lloyd took another swig of his drink, hating to even think about it. At least not right now while the victory was still fresh on his mind.

"Well, anyway, I'm going to head home," June said, grabbing her purse and standing. "I'll leave you two single gentlemen to ogle. See you guys tomorrow."

Lloyd and Steven ordered a second round of drinks after June left. They spoke briefly about an ongoing investigation before turning to more personal matters.

"So is it really getting serious between you and Courtney?" Steven lifted his screwdriver.

Lloyd stared at the question. "Yes, I guess it is."

They hadn't really talked about it, but Lloyd enjoyed her company in a way he hadn't any woman's in a long time. That had to be something. He sensed the same was true for her.

Steven laughed. "Come on, don't make it sound like a death sentence. I still wish my ex hadn't walked out on me and our son. I'd probably take her back in a Lake Barri minute."

Lloyd smiled. "Some things happen for the best. I'm sure there's another woman out there for you."

"When and if you find her, let me know. Not many women can handle being with a cop."

"Tell me about it." Lloyd wondered if Courtney could when all was said and done. They hadn't discussed the stress and strain of his job, its potential dangers or crazy hours. Maybe she would find that being a cop's steady date, or even wife, might be too much to handle.

I'd hate to put my heart and soul into this relationship only to lose Courtney once the going got tough.

Lloyd was nursing his drink when the soft voice got his attention.

"So are you on duty tonight or just here to have a good time?"

He looked up and saw a leggy female, somewhat familiar-looking, gazing down at him.

Glancing at Steven and back, Lloyd asked, "Do I know you?"

"Detective Vance, right?"

"Yeah." He was even more curious. "Who are you?"

"Gail Ramada. I took over the courses for Pilar Kendall. You visited our class—"

"Oh, yes." Lloyd was embarrassed that he didn't recognize her. Maybe it was because her hair—a dark curly shag—was down this time. And they were both out of their element. He introduced Gail to Steven. "I was hoping to get some leads in the hit-and-run at the college. And it looks like it worked," he said with amusement, eyeing Gail.

"I was so glad to hear that you found the driver," she told Lloyd.

"We all were." Lloyd only wished the culprit hadn't been one of Pilar's colleagues.

"Would you like to dance?"

His eyes widened. "Who, me…?"

She chuckled. "Yes. Unless, of course, you have two left feet?"

No, just a girlfriend who probably wouldn't approve. Lloyd favored Steven to help bail him out of this situation.

Instead he gave his support. "Go right ahead. I'll be fine on my own."

Lloyd's first thought was he should turn down the request. But why? There was no harm in dancing at a club with a pretty lady. Besides, Courtney wasn't here and he considered it good practice.

He gave Gail a half smile. "Sure, why not."

"It feels kind of weird being here," Courtney said as she and Olivia entered the Train Stop. This was her first time back since the night she was supposed to meet Pilar there. Instead she'd met Lloyd and had never seen her cousin alive again.

"I know." Olivia frowned. "Don't think about it. We're here to have fun, remember?"

"Yes, you're right." Courtney bit her lip, determined not to get upset about something she had no control over. The important thing was that Pilar's killer was now behind bars. *So just relax and enjoy the atmosphere.*

"Let's go find a table."

Soon they were seated and sipping Pina Coladas.

"I think I could get used to these ladies' nights out," Olivia said, bobbing her head to the sounds of R. Kelly.

"Oh, really?" Courtney's lashes fluttered. "Already tiring of your man?"

"Never. There's nothing wrong with gal pals spending time together away from the books and without men looking over our shoulders."

"Agreed." *Truthfully, I'd rather be here with Lloyd— or somewhere more private. But since he had other plans, it's nice to hang with Olivia now that Pilar's gone.*

Olivia's eyes grew. "Uh-oh. Maybe I spoke too soon…"

"Meaning?"

"I thought you said Lloyd was out drinking with people from work?"

"He is," Courtney stated.

"Unless my eyesight is going bad, it looks like your boyfriend found a better way to entertain himself."

Following the path of her gaze, Courtney looked to

the dance floor and saw Lloyd dancing. Or more like standing there and allowing his partner to do all the work, up close and personal. She had her back to Lloyd and was brushing her bottom lewdly against his body, practically giving him a lap dance while standing. And he certainly looked like he was enjoying it.

Courtney had been so startled by the performance that only now did she focus on the woman's face, recognizing her as none other than Gail Ramada.

Chapter 18

Lloyd did a double take when he spotted Courtney at a table. Feeling the searing heat from her eyes, he pretended not to notice and finished the dance. *It's not like she caught me in bed with another woman. So why do I feel like it?*

When the song ended, he walked off the dance floor with Gail. "Thanks for the dance."

She beamed. "Anytime, Detective."

Probably not. "I have to go talk to someone."

Gail's brow furrowed. "Guess I'll see you later, then."

He offered her a weak smile and made his way to the table occupied by Courtney and Olivia. *I can only imagine who they've been talking about.*

"Courtney," Lloyd said sweetly. "What are you doing here?"

"What does it look like—having a drink with a friend." Her lips tightened. "Same thing I thought you were doing."

"I am." He glanced over at his table and saw it empty. "Steven is here, and June left a little while ago."

Courtney glared. "So you thought you'd just play the field again since your girlfriend was at home."

"C'mon, you're overreacting. It was just a dance."

"That wasn't *just* a dance. She was all over you—like making love on the dance floor."

Lloyd glanced at Olivia and watched her avert her eyes before focusing on Courtney again. "That was nothing like making love, as you should know *all* too well."

"Why her?" Courtney questioned.

"Why who?"

"Gail Ramada."

He cocked a brow. "You two know each other?"

"She took over Pilar's classes, and now I see you cozying up to her on the dance floor, almost as though she were the reincarnation of Pilar."

Lloyd smirked. "That's ridiculous."

"Is it?"

"Yes! I met Gail during the course of the hit-and-run investigation. We're not friends. Or even acquaintances. She asked me to dance and I agreed just for the sake of it. I wasn't fooling around behind your back or pining for Pilar with another woman." *I can't believe I'm being forced to explain myself over something so harmless.*

Courtney heard Lloyd but was in no mood to listen. Except for her husband, she hadn't had much luck with men. Still, Lloyd had given her no reason to distrust him. Until now. All she could think now was that he was more interested in playing the field than being in a committed relationship. She was not the type of woman who thought nothing of sharing a man with other women. She needed someone who understood that.

Was Lloyd that man?

She met his steady gaze. "You know what? Why don't you go back over there with your friend or coworker and leave me to enjoy my drink with Olivia."

Lloyd's nostrils grew. "Are you sure that's what you really want?"

Courtney wasn't certain but couldn't back down now. Otherwise she might never have the strength to stand up for her convictions.

"Yes, I'm sure it is for now."

"Fine. See you later."

Lloyd nodded curtly at Olivia and walked away. He'd always had trouble trying to figure out women. Now was no exception. Courtney was being totally unreasonable on a day in which she should have been elated. Instead of finding satisfaction in the apprehension of a hit-and-run driver, she chose to bicker over his dancing with a woman at a club.

Since I didn't do anything wrong, why should I have to apologize? She's acting like I'm her husband instead of her boyfriend, who is still single, technically speaking, and free to dance with someone if I choose to.

Getting on his case for that, like the jealous woman from hell, definitely got Lloyd's attention but also set off warning bells. Had they rushed into this thing too soon following Pilar's death?

Was Courtney looking for him to be a clone of her late husband?

By the time he sat back down, Lloyd was thinking that maybe they needed to cool things for a while. *Isn't that what Courtney was implying?*

Or would being apart only make them miss each other that much more?

"Wow, I didn't see that coming," remarked Olivia, sipping on her cocktail.

Courtney eyed her sharply. "Neither did I."

"Don't you think you went a little overboard with your reaction?"

I don't know. "Not really. I saw the same thing you did. Lloyd was clearly enjoying Gail rubbing herself up against him and calling it dancing. That's not what I expect from someone I've been dating steadily. How would you feel if it were Jeremy?"

Olivia paused. "Probably just as you did," she admitted, "hurt, confused, uncertain."

"I thought we had something special," Courtney said. "He's made me feel alive for the first time since Joseph died. But that doesn't mean I should simply ignore the reality that Lloyd might not feel the same way. Tonight I saw a man who seemed more than happy to be single again without a girlfriend cramping his style."

Am I overanalyzing the situation? Is this simply a case of a jealous girlfriend without justification? Does a sexual dance really mean Lloyd wants the best of both worlds?

"So what are you going to do?" Olivia leaned forward curiously.

Courtney thought about the question. She didn't want to break things off with Lloyd prematurely. *I don't really want to lose him*. But forgetting what she saw wasn't an option, either.

Maybe it wasn't really that big a deal. She didn't exactly catch him cheating, per se.

Was there such a thing as mental infidelity?

Lloyd may have been innocent of any physical wrongdoing. But what about the next time? Maybe he would take it one step further with Gail or some other woman if the opportunity arose and Lloyd felt he could get away with it.

Can I really be with someone I'm not sure I can trust...even if I don't want to lose him?

She looked up at Olivia through watery eyes and blinked. "I don't know—"

"Just promise me you won't make any decisions before talking to Lloyd about your feelings."

Courtney wiped a tear from her cheek. Was there really anything to talk about? Would he only say what she wanted to hear?

I need to know that he wants more out of this relationship than convenient get-togethers and steamy sex. Or is that asking too much?

"I won't," she agreed to Olivia's request.

Chapter 19

Lloyd must have driven around the block half a dozen times, circling Courtney's house. The better part of him wanted to knock on her door and see if they could clear the air. But the other side felt that groveling would be counterproductive. The last thing he needed was to appear weak and at fault for doing what amounted to nothing that should threaten a relationship.

So how do I make things right for us again?

In the end he decided it was best to leave Courtney alone for now. Maybe tomorrow they would both see things differently.

Or perhaps the divide would grow even deeper?

In bed that night, Lloyd had a restless but pleasing

sleep. He dreamed about making love to Courtney as kiss-and-make-up sex. It was wonderful till he woke up and realized none of it had been real.

Damn. What type of hold does she have on me that can even penetrate my subconscious thoughts?

Lloyd wished to hell he didn't long for Courtney's touch and to be deep inside her while they passionately kissed. She was one of a kind and he couldn't get her off his mind, even when he wanted to. He didn't want to invest his emotions in someone who didn't seem to have enough confidence in herself and their relationship to withstand something so innocent as a dance.

Would I have reacted the same way had the situation been reversed?

He couldn't answer that. He knew Courtney wasn't the type to just throw herself at men. So why wouldn't he trust her if someone at a club asked her to dance, even if it seemed sexual in nature? Wasn't that par for the course with dancing these days?

Since Courtney was a beautiful woman, he had to expect that in his absence men would want to dance with her. And it would be her right to have fun then.

So why shouldn't it be same the other way around?

Lloyd chewed on that thought till he fell asleep again.

The next day Lloyd was back at work, wrapping up the department's case against Gordon McNair. Now it was up to the district attorney's office to make sure it stood up, in the event the suspect sought to recant his confession or otherwise refused to play ball in owning up to the hit-and-run.

Lloyd met with Steven in a conference room prior to an update on his ongoing investigation of a teenager's death.

"Hope I didn't blow it last night for you, buddy." Steven narrowed his eyes.

Lloyd recalled that his friend had encouraged him to dance with Gail. "You didn't. Neither of us knew Courtney would show up." Or act like it was the end of the world.

"So I suppose you're in her doghouse?"

Lloyd sighed. "Yeah, I guess you could say that."

"Chances are she'll get over it in a day or two."

"That's just it. There shouldn't be anything to get over."

"Hey, you're singing to the band, man. Guess Courtney really must have her hooks into you and was simply marking her territory."

Lloyd smiled faintly. "Sounds like you've been down that road?"

"Who hasn't? I wouldn't sweat it if I were you. At least you have someone who isn't afraid to make her feelings known. Unlike my ex, who waited till she boiled over before bolting for the door."

Lloyd wondered just how strong things were between him and Courtney. Or how weak. Would she let him back in? Or throw what they had away in the blink of an eye without sufficient cause?

* * *

"I think I lost my perspective." The words sprang from Courtney's mouth in being honest about her reaction to Lloyd and the sexy dance. Her listening ear was Olivia, whose house Courtney had dropped by that afternoon.

"How so?" Olivia stopped drinking green tea.

"By putting too much faith in Lloyd as marriage material." Courtney grabbed a homemade oatmeal cookie and bit off a small piece thoughtfully. "After Pilar died, I allowed myself to become too dependent on him as a friend and lover. Don't know if I was still trying to get Joseph out of my system or simply felt I needed someone who was totally into me. Either way, I put that all on Lloyd. Now I realize it wasn't fair. We have great chemistry, but that's about all. He's clearly not looking for anything lasting between us. Or at least I'm getting that vibe."

"You may be right about that," Olivia said, "or you could be dead wrong. I brought the subject up to Jeremy last night and he thinks it was no big deal."

Courtney's lashes flickered. "Easy for him to say."

"He feels that all men like to mess around, especially when they're trying to impress their buddies. Most of it is harmless, he says, so long as it stays on the dance floor."

"What if it doesn't?"

"Then that's a whole different can of worms. But since that never happened, there's no reason to even go there."

Courtney swallowed. "So you think I should just forget it and be happy it's my bed Lloyd's spending a good deal of his time in?"

"I didn't say that. I just think you should give it some thought before you let a good thing get away."

"Oh. So now you think he's a *good* thing?"

Olivia chuckled. "Don't you? C'mon, girl, I see the way you two look at each other, and can only guess what goes on behind closed doors. I doubt he's doing the same thing with anyone else."

Courtney couldn't help but think about their intense lovemaking, giving her a hot flash. It was hard to imagine Lloyd being so sexually attentive with Gail or anyone else. That was beside the point, though. She'd never accused him of being unfaithful. But somehow allowing another woman to use him as a sex prop seemed almost as bad.

"I hear what you're saying." She gazed at Olivia. "Yes, we have a great sex life. Or had. But I need more out of a relationship, and I'm not sure I can get that from Lloyd."

"Have you shared your views with him?"

"I think right now we just need a little time apart," Courtney said. "Which is partly why I'm going up to the cabin to spend a couple of days—alone."

Olivia's eyes rolled. "At this time of year?"

"What better time? It's beautiful up there right now, and the winter weather is still weeks off. I'll be fine. Besides, it was one of the last places Pilar and I really hung out together. Now that the man who ran her down is in custody, I can sort of put final closure there and get some work done at same time."

Olivia grabbed a cookie and bit off a nice chunk. "Sure you can't use some company? I need a break from town."

"Not this time." Courtney flashed a smile, appreciating her friendship even more these days with Pilar gone. "But you're free to use the cabin whenever you like—even bring Jeremy along. Right now I just need to be by myself, away from Lloyd and Lake Barri."

By the time I return, I hope to have a new perspective on things and we can go from there.

Lloyd caught June as she was heading out of her office for home.

"Can you spare a few minutes?"

"For you, anything." She smiled playfully. "What's up?"

"I need some advice." June was one of the few women Lloyd had established a camaraderie with since moving to Lake Barri. She seemed a good bet to solicit an opinion on his current predicament with Courtney.

They stepped into his office, and Lloyd waited for June to take a seat before sitting beside her.

"I may have screwed things up with Courtney," he told her.

"How?"

He explained what happened last night after June left the club. "I don't feel like I stepped over the line. Unfortunately Courtney sees it differently. She thinks I somehow betrayed whatever it is we have."

June folded her arms. "And what do you have exactly?"

Good question. "As far as I know, we have great chemistry and get along well. I don't want to lose her—not over something that shouldn't be a deal breaker."

"In that case I suggest you do the little things women love as your way of apologizing for hurt feelings—even if your male pride would rather take a stand and let her make the first move."

"Such as?"

"You can start out with flowers. They sell some great I'm Sorry gift bouquets. Roses are always a winner, but giving her something like Alstroemerias or Persian Violets would make it seem like you put more effort into the apology."

Lloyd grinned. "I didn't realize you were a florist."

"You asked." She smiled back. "I do happen to have a green thumb when I'm not working or five months pregnant."

"I can do that. Anything else?"

"Does she like chocolate?"

Lloyd mused. "I'm not sure."

"I'll take that as a yes. Most women devour the stuff. Get her an assorted box of chocolates so she knows how sweet you are on her."

"That all?" He hoped this wouldn't get too expensive on a cop's salary.

"Just give her some added attention to show how much you care." June tapped his knee. "Believe me, works every time with my husband. If your relationship with Courtney is half as tight as you think, you should get the same results."

"Thanks, I appreciate your help."

"That's what occasional partners are for. Now can I go? The baby's kicking again. I think he's telling me it's time to eat."

"Yes, get out of here."

For some reason Lloyd loved hearing about June's unborn child and the symbiotic relationship they had. He wanted to be connected like that to his own child someday.

The next day Lloyd picked up the flowers and chocolates, as well as a big card expressing regret for the circumstances that put a strain on things between him and Courtney.

He showed up at her house and there was no sign of Courtney's car. Damn. So much for a total surprise.

Lloyd lifted his cell phone to ring Courtney but had second thoughts and aborted the plan. The last thing he needed was for her to hang up on him. Or worse, tell him to get lost. Some things could only be resolved face-to-face.

I'll swing by Olivia's place. Maybe Courtney's there or Olivia can tell me where to find her.

It had only been a couple of days since their falling out, yet to Lloyd it seemed like a lifetime or two. He was determined to do something about that for both their sakes.

Chapter 20

Courtney was stuck in traffic, apparently not the only person heading out of town. She wondered if they were all also leaving to reassess their lives or reflect on a loss, and hoping to come back refreshed?

She used the pause in movement to check her cell phone. Though Courtney had purposefully kept if off to avoid talking to Lloyd, she had hoped he would leave a message to say how much he missed her.

Courtney frowned when she saw there were no new messages.

Guess he doesn't miss me as much as I do him.

Not that Courtney seriously expected anything different. After all, it was she who had set the separation in motion and headed for the hills.

Lloyd apparently was more than happy to accept that without much protest.

Have I sent him away for good? Oh well, maybe it's for the best. If we can't agree on rules of behavior when out on the town, how on earth can we ever make a successful go at it for the long haul as a couple?

A horn beeping caught Courtney's attention. She pressed down on the accelerator and started moving again.

Soon the logjam had eased and she was cruising down I-25. Courtney noted a car on the shoulder, the driver leaning against it, apparently out of gas. She considered for a moment offering the man a ride but thought better. Since he had a cell phone up to his ear, she was sure help was on the way.

Her thoughts returned to making the most of the weekend and getting back on the right track. She was a little worried about the threat of an early snowfall in the foothills. A little R & R didn't include an adventure in slipping and sliding or being stuck in the middle of nowhere.

It wasn't long before Courtney had exited the highway and headed toward Cougar Springs, an out-of-the-way resort community nestled in the Rocky Mountains. She drove past rows of Ponderosa pines and over curving roads, finally arriving at the cabin.

Purchased by the grandparents of Courtney and Pilar forty years ago, the two eventually inherited the rustic log cabin, using it as an escape from their normal lives and, in Courtney's case, an ideal place to write.

She ambled down a cobblestone walkway surrounded by little princess spirea. After unlocking the door, Courtney went in, wondering if it might have been smarter to remain in Lake Barri and deal with Lloyd head-on instead of running away.

Lloyd pulled his car up to Olivia's house. He had been there once when she'd invited him and Courtney to dinner. He enjoyed spending time with Courtney's friends, particularly Jeremy, who seemed like a nice guy he could hang out with.

Lloyd frowned when he didn't see Courtney's car. Hoping Olivia could tell him where to find her, he went up to the house and knocked.

Jeremy opened the door and greeted Lloyd like an old friend.

"Come on in, man."

Inside Lloyd caught Olivia coming down the stairs. "Hey there," he said evenly.

"Hi, Lloyd." She gave him a tentative look. "If you're looking for Courtney, she's not here."

Now why do you suppose I would be looking for her? "I thought about calling her but figured she wouldn't pick up."

Olivia remained mute.

"Do you know where she is?"

Olivia's eyes darted to Jeremy and back. "She just wants to be alone right now."

"That's cool," Lloyd said, though not meaning it.

"Look, I just need to talk to her for a few minutes. If she tells me to get lost after that, I will."

Jeremy took Olivia's hand. "Maybe you should let them work this out."

"Maybe they will," she said. "But right now Courtney doesn't want to go there. As her best friend, I have to respect her wishes."

"So you do know where she is?" Lloyd gave her a hard look.

"I didn't say that."

Oh, yes you did, in essence. He wondered if Courtney had actually gone to Florida a couple of weeks before Thanksgiving—without him.

Realizing he couldn't make Olivia tell him anything, Lloyd could only hope to persuade her. "I messed things up with Courtney—if dancing at a club with someone who meant nothing to me qualifies as such. We had a good thing going, and I don't want to see it derailed because something got blown out of proportion. If Courtney and I can just talk this through—"

Olivia touched her hair. "I understand what you're saying and hope it works out between you two. I just don't want to get caught in the middle of your spat. All I can tell you is that Courtney should be back in a few days and you can contact her then."

Lloyd wanted to rant and rave, but what good would that do? Obviously Courtney didn't want to see him and had left explicit instructions with Olivia to that effect.

Well, can't say I didn't try like hell. Guess the ball is in Courtney's court now.

"Thanks for your time," he told Olivia politely. "See you two later."

"I'll walk you out," Jeremy said.

Lloyd wondered how things had become so strained between him and Courtney in such a short time. Could be things weren't meant to work out for them in the long run. Or was that just a cop-out?

"Sorry about that." Jeremy twisted his lips as they neared Lloyd's car.

"Yeah, so am I," he said. "I suppose I'll see Courtney when I see her."

Jeremy paused before lowering his voice. "I'm probably going out on a limb here, and Olivia will be really pissed, but I think you and Courtney need to talk sooner than later. She went to spend a couple days at her cabin."

Lloyd's brow lifted. The cabin was news to him. "You know where the cabin's located?"

"Only that it's somewhere in Cougar Springs."

"Okay, I should be able to find it." Lloyd patted his shoulder. "Thanks, I owe you one."

"Good luck."

Lloyd had a feeling it would take more than luck to win Courtney's trust again. Whether or not he was up to the task remained to be seen.

* * *

The cabin was just as cozy as Courtney remembered with its cedar furniture, pine floors and large windows offering amazing views. There was electricity, running water and pretty much all the comforts of home minus the headaches. It was the first time she'd been there since Pilar's death, making her all the more nostalgic.

I wish we could've spent a few more times here together, Pilar. Sometimes I feel so lonely without you, even though my work keeps me very busy. Olivia is a great friend, as you know, but can't take the place of my favorite cuz.

Courtney thought about Lloyd. Part of her wished he'd come to Cougar Springs, too, although the very reason for her being there was to put some distance between them. Overall she believed it was for the best.

Fresh, clean mountain air and tranquility was just what she needed to clear her head.

She opened up the refrigerator and saw a few leftovers that had to go right in the trash. Looked like a trip to the store was in order.

Courtney unpacked a few things and freshened up. For some reason she suddenly thought about Alaska. She could picture a similar setting in the mountains there with Lloyd acting as her sexy tour guide.

She realized that it might all be nothing more than a pipe dream at this point. *I can't make him want more out of this relationship than he does. I'm not into head games. Or competing with others for a man's attention.*

Grabbing her purse, Courtney was out the door.

Lloyd drove on the highway toward the mountain town. It was easy enough to track down the cabin's address on his work computer. Yahoo did the rest, providing a map and directions.

In the passenger seat were the quickly wilting flowers, box of chocolates and card. *Don't know if any of them will do me any good if Courtney refuses to talk.*

He felt the trip was well worth the risk. Or the woman. They had come too far to give up without a fight. And he'd always been a fighter ever since his father walked out on them and Lloyd was forced to be a man much sooner that he had wanted.

By comparison, he figured getting back on Courtney's good side should be a piece of cake.

Light snow had begun to fall as had been forecast with a cold front moving through the area. The idea of a blast of winter did not deter Lloyd. Quite the contrary. After being used to far worse in Alaska, he was prepared to deal with whatever came his way.

Except for being rejected by Courtney.

Arriving at the cabin, Lloyd saw no sign of Courtney's Tribeca. *Could I have actually gotten here first?*

He left the car and went up to the door, noting some firewood stacked near the side of the house. A whiff of perfume he recognized as Courtney's favorite, which tantalized him whenever she wore it, told Lloyd she had made it to Cougar Springs. He knocked, but figured she had probably gone to town to get food.

Lloyd twisted the knob and found it wasn't locked. *Guess I'll just invite myself in and hope I don't get arrested for breaking and entering.*

It was a bit musty inside but otherwise seemed like the perfect hideaway. He was sure there were plenty of stories in the cabin's history. Hopefully Courtney would share some with him.

Assuming she didn't toss him out on his rear and back to Lake Barri with the issues between them left unresolved.

Chapter 21

Courtney carried her grocery bags into the cabin, feeling a chill. Perhaps she would make a fire and relax with cup of hot chocolate, then do a little work and break into some serious reverie.

Courtney poured water into the kettle and was about to turn the burner on when she heard a knock at the door. She assumed it was someone who had gotten lost or maybe a neighbor seeking to borrow firewood or something.

The last person Courtney expected to find at the door was Lloyd, giving her a start.

"What are you doing here…?"

He half grinned. "Came to bring you this—"

She hadn't even noticed the bouquet of flowers and box of chocolates.

"I'm sorry the flowers lost some of their luster during the trip, but it's the thought that counts."

Courtney would have agreed in most circumstances, except for the fact that no one was supposed to know she was there—least of all Lloyd. She studied him. He was dressed warmly in a heavy jacket, jeans and boots, similar to her own attire.

"How did you find me?" The answer was obvious to Courtney: Olivia. *I'm going to kill her for this.*

"Actually it wasn't all that hard. I'm a cop, remember?"

Courtney doubted she could ever forget, along with the fact he had a wandering eye.

Still, Lloyd had tracked her down and had gone out of his way to do so, meaning he must care about her. No reason to send him back out in the cold right away.

She took the flowers. "I'll go put these in some water."

Lloyd noted that she'd kept the door open, which he took as an invitation to enter. A step in the right direction. Now he only hoped they could settle their differences like civilized adults and move forward.

Courtney put the vase on the octagon table, fully expecting the flowers to spring back to life. Whether their relationship could or should was a different matter.

"Hope you like almond caramel clusters and dark chocolates?" Lloyd said.

"Much more than I should. Not very good for my waistline but thanks, anyway." She took the box, promising herself not to devour the whole box before returning to Lake Barri.

He smiled sexily. "I suspect most women would kill for your waistline."

Courtney could not deny he was as charming as ever in making a woman feel special. She wondered what sweet words he'd whispered to Gail.

Do I care?

She met his eyes. "I didn't hear your car drive up."

"I parked in the back. Didn't want to give you a heart attack."

"You nearly did."

"Sorry about that. I was going to call but—"

"My phone was off anyway, so it wouldn't have mattered."

"I wanted to do this in person, plus it gave me an excuse to take a personal day."

She put her hands on her hips. "I thought we agreed to cool things for a while?"

He cocked a brow. "Really? I was under the impression we only had a minor disagreement and it was time to put that behind us."

"Did you?" Courtney couldn't help but flash a tiny smile though she considered the situation anything but funny.

"Seemed like a good idea."

She looked away from his intense stare. "You really didn't have to drive all the way up here to—"

"It was no problem," he cut in. "I just wanted to see

you and saw no reason why we couldn't get everything out in the open and back to where we were."

Courtney faced him again. And just where were they? More importantly, where did they go from here?

"I was just about to make myself a cup of hot chocolate," she told him. "Would you like one?"

"I'd love a cup." Lloyd was happy that she hadn't asked him to leave. Not yet, anyway.

They sat at the table sipping cocoa in silence until Lloyd felt this had gone far enough. There was no reason for them to be at arm's length, figuratively or literally. He was not about to let their relationship slowly disintegrate.

"Look, I'm sorry if Gail got a little crazy with her dancing. I think she had too much to drink."

Courtney snickered. "What was your excuse?"

"I have none. Just wanted to get on the floor and dance—sort of pat myself on the back for making an arrest in Pilar's hit-and-run. I probably would've danced by myself before long." He gazed at her expressively. "For what it's worth, whether you'd been there or not, I saved the most important dance for you."

Courtney rolled her eyes. Cute, if not original. How does one stay angry at a man who can so smoothly deliver such lines?

"So maybe I overreacted a little. Why don't we just forget it?"

"Now what were we talking about?" Lloyd gave her

a comical grin. He wanted to build on the momentum. "I have to say that I never pictured you owning a cabin up in the mountains."

"And why not?" She looked at him with a straight face.

"Guess I never took you for the outdoorsy, back-to-nature type."

"Who says I am?" She chuckled. "Pilar and I inherited the cabin from our grandparents who were very much into the wilderness and mountains. We talked about selling from time to time, but decided to keep it for getaways and even to pass on to our own children."

She paused on that note and Lloyd felt her pain in knowing that Pilar would never have that opportunity. But there was still hope for Courtney having children to leave the place to someday.

"I think it's a good thing to keep the cabin," he agreed. "Certainly seems well preserved and a great place to enjoy some down time. I'm sure Pilar would concur."

Courtney fought back tears. "I'm really glad you caught the guy who ran her down."

"I was sure we would, sooner or later. Sorry you had to go through this."

"So am I." She took a deep breath. "I met him…"

Lloyd looked at her with arched brows. "The driver?"

She nodded. "Yes. He was at my signing at the mall with his daughter. I signed a book for her."

"What the hell?" His forehead furrowed. "Do you think he knew you were related to Pilar?"

"Probably not." Courtney chose to give him the benefit of the doubt. "He was just being a loving father."

"Yeah, right—one who hid behind his daughter while knowing he'd killed a woman and was wanted by the police."

In no way was Courtney excusing his actions. How could she? "I'm just glad Pilar didn't have to suffer long, or be left as a vegetable or otherwise unable to live a normal life."

That was something Lloyd felt grateful for, too. Though he only knew Pilar for a short while, something told him they would have ended up as great friends. Lloyd was sure Pilar would never have been hurting in the romance department, either, given her attractiveness and outgoing personality.

He focused on Courtney, who seemed to be absorbed in her own thoughts. He stood and reached out to her.

"Would you like to dance?"

Courtney arched a brow. "There's no music playing." Not that she couldn't turn on the stereo.

"We can make our own music."

Feeling compelled, she took his hand and was pulled up. Lloyd held her in his arms and they began to move slowly to imaginary music.

Silence turned into real music as Lloyd began to croon a Seal tune and effortlessly switched into one by Usher. Courtney got caught up in the music, as impressed by Lloyd's ability to sing in tune as she was with the man himself.

Feeling relaxed in his arms, Courtney actually surprised herself by singing along.

Lloyd gave an approving smile. He loved the way Courtney sang and could listen to her melodic voice all day. He inhaled her sweet and sensual scent, closing his eyes to enhance his senses.

Holding her waist, Lloyd pulled back and gazed down into Courtney's desire-filled eyes. He looked at her mouth, opened ever so slightly, moist, glossy and ready to be taken. He positioned his head and kissed her.

Courtney felt she would melt on the spot from the searing heat of Lloyd's burning kiss. Her legs grew weak as she clung to his neck.

When he gets like this, the man is totally irresistible and makes me powerless.

Her body on fire, she put her all into the kiss, wanting to taste as much of Lloyd as he would allow.

Consumed by the embers burning wildly within, Lloyd kept up his part of the bargain as their open mouths crushed into each other's with the desperation of starved lovers, searching through tongues and teeth for every treasure to be found.

Lloyd put his hands to Courtney's breasts, caressing her tautened nipples with gentle yet steady persuasion. This sent electric waves of ecstasy to her brain, then slowly down her body, culminating between her legs. She gasped as if he were already inside her making love, so intense was the feeling.

With his breathing labored and erection begging for

release, Lloyd spoke hoarsely into Courtney's mouth, "I need you more than ever."

Trying to catch her own erratic breath without breaking the kiss, Courtney let body language speak for her, pressing against him fervently.

With that, Lloyd scooped her into his arms and went to the bedroom. There he began to undress her with his eyes and sure hands as Courtney returned the favor in rapid fashion. The buildup of adrenaline had her heart pounding with thrilling anticipation.

She climbed onto the log bed and waited for Lloyd to join. He did so without missing a beat, slipping on a condom in one fluid motion. He immediately put his face down into the valley of her breasts, licking tenderly, giving Courtney instant chill bumps.

Lloyd focused on Courtney's nipples, expertly taunting them with his mouth and tongue, wanting to enjoy tasting as much as titillating her.

Courtney felt as if she would burst from the raw sensations radiating from her nipples. She suppressed an urge to cry out and instead ran her hands through Lloyd's hair to let him know how utterly delightful it made her feel.

Lloyd heard her silent satisfaction, heightening his own nearly overpowering desires. Sliding a hand down her moist thigh, he put a finger between her legs and found Courtney was very wet.

Just what I'd hoped. She's relaxing and turned on, letting herself go to that special place.

He stimulated her for a time, burrowing a couple of

fingers inside, watching Courtney's reaction. Lloyd swallowed thickly but refused to succumb to his almost urgent needs. He rained a torrent of hot kisses down her body, very slowly and deliberately, till he reached his destination.

Lloyd drank Courtney's enticing nectar and put his mouth over her clitoris, which was erect, exposed.

Courtney was woozy from the exquisite foreplay, wrapping her legs around Lloyd's neck. A guttural moan escaped her as she climaxed onto his face.

"Lloyd..." she yowled, totally caught up in and enjoying the moment.

Hearing his name during Courtney's orgasm drove Lloyd crazy. He couldn't wait a second longer to relieve his yearnings and prolong hers. He lifted up, licking her sweet moisture from his lips.

"Kiss me," Courtney demanded, wanting to feel his mouth upon hers as they made love.

She covered his lips with kisses and stuck her tongue inside, tasting a mixture of herself and him. The effect was maddening, making Courtney feel they really did belong together. And no one could stand in their way.

Lloyd spread Courtney's legs and propelled himself into her. He felt her ankles hook around his, the slickness of their bodies as he went deeper and deeper inside. His desire for Courtney had never been so great.

Courtney arched her hips and winced with pleasure at each thrust. She peppered his chin, neck, ears, nose and eyes with kisses, wanting to kiss his entire being.

He had brought her to new heights, and she couldn't help but want to give back the same.

The primordial sounds of them slamming into each other like modern-day gladiators rocked the bed back and forth.

Left and right.

Up and down.

Courtney bit into Lloyd's shoulder while strapping one leg across his buttock, unable to control herself or slow down the intensity of their intimacy.

So engrossed was he in the passionate lovemaking, Lloyd barely felt Courtney's teeth puncture his skin. His orgasm was coming and he wanted nothing more than to feel its thunderous bolt of lightning strike while wedged deep within Courtney.

It was what she wanted, too, as Courtney held back another sizzling climax, knowing it would be that much more fulfilling when they achieved it together.

Their bodies became one in that moment of rapture, with Courtney and Lloyd sharing a prolonged burst of shuddering satisfaction. They panted, murmured, moaned, laughed, cried, hummed and shouted each other's names.

Afterward they lay spent in each other's arms, their breathing slowly returning to normal. Heartbeats fell back into rhythm. Equilibrium was restored to a level where they could come to grips with time and place.

Lloyd kissed Courtney again, long and hard, glad to be back in her good graces. He still wasn't sure where the future would take them, but wanted it to be long and far. She was the woman Lloyd never wanted to get out of his system.

If he played his cards right, Courtney would be the one who didn't get away.

Reciprocating the kiss, Courtney only wished the magic spell could last forever. As reality began to set in, she had to face the fact that Lloyd's feelings for her might never go as far as hers for him.

Could she settle for having an alluring Alaskan lover and nothing more?

Chapter 22

"What was your husband like?"

Courtney was still wrapped in Lloyd's comforting arms, naked atop the comforter, when he asked the question out of nowhere.

"This is hardly the time to compare," she said, ill at ease.

Lloyd chuckled. "I wasn't asking how he performed in bed." Though the thought of how he stacked up to her late husband in that department had entered his mind.

She looked up at him. "What are you asking?" She really didn't want to discuss Joseph with her lover, terrific though Lloyd was.

"Just wondered what type of man he was. Obviously a genius, for starters."

She cocked a brow. "Genius…?"

"The man was smart enough to get you to walk down the aisle. I'd say that qualifies as genius."

She laughed. "You're too much."

"Just telling it like it is." Lloyd kissed her smooth, soft shoulder. He was envious that someone had come along before him and swept her off those lovely feet.

Courtney ran her toes up the side of his leg, flattered as always when he complimented her like that. She wondered if Lloyd was the marrying type. Or was he more comfortable watching others tie the knot while maintaining his own independence from that type of commitment?

"Joseph was a good, hardworking man," she said. "He enjoyed being introspective, watching shows on public broadcasting, fishing and reading historical books."

Lloyd touched her breast, still damp from lovemaking. "Did he treat you well?"

"Yes, as well as he knew how. Joseph was not really an affectionate person," she admitted. "But he loved me and wanted me to be happy."

Lloyd wanted her to be happy, too—and loved. He felt he could give her that happiness and that what they had was surely on the brink of love. He didn't want to take the term lightly, having seen firsthand how hollow such words could be. When they had reached the point where it was appropriate to discuss love and devotion, he would be ready.

"Glad to hear that," he told her.

"And what about your last girlfriend?" Courtney asked, wondering if she was the Ms. Wrong he had mentioned earlier. "What was she like?"

Lloyd sighed, mulling that one over. He had once thought Evangeline Klass was the one. Till Lloyd saw a side of her he wanted no part of. Fortunately she had already turned her sights toward someone who could be more easily wrapped around her little finger.

"Moody, spoiled, self-centered and even a little egotistical."

Courtney laughed, feeling strangely relieved. "Is that all?"

"Isn't it enough?"

"Sounds like many women I know, present company excluded."

"Maybe the *moody* would apply," Lloyd half joked.

She hit him. "Oh, you think so, do you?"

"It's a good moodiness."

Her eyes flashed with amusement. "Digging yourself into a deeper hole."

"So was Joseph a better lover…?"

Courtney chortled, realizing he had cleverly diverted one subject with one that was equally contentious. In truth, she doubted anyone could be so thorough a lover as Lloyd. But since he probably already knew that, she saw no need to further bolster his ego.

She kissed him and ran fingernails gently across his chest. "Let's just say you have nothing to worry about in that department."

He grinned. "Care to back that up? Or shall I?"

She hummed, feeling arousal take hold of her body once more. "Maybe we both can."

"Now you're speaking my language," Lloyd said. He was definitely ready for another round.

Courtney opened her eyes, having fallen asleep after making love again to Lloyd. She expected to find him beside her, but the spot was empty. Had his presence been nothing more than a figment of her imagination?

She sniffed, smelling his gloriously appealing masculine scent all over her, and smiled. The hours of exploring each other thoroughly really had happened.

Suddenly all the reasons for escaping to the cabin had been thrown into doubt. Her misgivings had mostly been answered, even if she was still uncertain as to where this was headed. She supposed it was best not to overthink things and show some patience—not usually her strong point.

She got up and put on a robe, padded across the floor and out the door.

She found Lloyd kneeling over the fireplace, putting logs in.

"Thought maybe you had decided to head back to Lake Barri."

He smiled up at her. "Not quite. I figured I'd hang out here with you for the rest of the day and night, if you'll have me."

Courtney glowed, imagining how they were likely to spend much of that time. "You're welcome to stay. But what about work tomorrow? Another personal day?"

"I wish. Actually, I traded shifts with another detective. Besides, I wouldn't want to get greedy and monopolize all your time here."

Even if the thought of monopolizing each other was appealing in many ways, Courtney did need to get some work in, as well as add a little more closure to Pilar's death. Then there was the reality that Lloyd had a life, too, apart from Courtney. She would never want to take his job away. No matter how much the idea of working in law enforcement may have concerned her—the unpredictable hours and possible danger.

She wrapped her arms around Lloyd's neck as he built the fire, already feeling its warmth. "You must be hungry…for food?"

He stood up and kissed her. "I think we've both built up an appetite. What did you have in mind?"

"Since the cupboards were bare when I arrived, and I wasn't expecting company when I went out for a few things, why don't we eat in town? I noticed a nice little bistro that might be fun to check out."

"Sounds like a plan. But what about the fire?"

Courtney licked her lips sensually. "The place should be nice and toasty by the time we get back. If not, there are other ways to start a fire."

Lloyd liked the sound of that. He had played his

hand right, not only in coming after Courtney today, but knowing from the first time he laid eyes on her that she was worth pursuing. He was willing to do whatever it took to keep this thing going strong between them.

Something told him that Courtney's feelings were just as strong.

Chapter 23

By Sunday afternoon the snow that had fallen over the weekend had all but vanished. Meaning the roads were clear and Courtney would have no trouble heading back to Lake Barri. Before locking up the place, she took one final look around the cabin, remembering the great times she'd had there with Pilar and, more recently, Lloyd. Courtney wasn't sure when she would return, only that coming here had achieved her objectives and more. Now it was time to get back to the real world and see if the reconnection with Lloyd would last. Or if they'd end up as nothing more than friends with sexual benefits.

On Monday morning Courtney e-mailed the manuscript she'd completed to her editor, hoping it would be a winner. Every writer's greatest fear was that what seemed like a solid effort, if not a masterpiece, would be considered terrible by those who counted most. While Courtney had never gotten a stinging rebuke of her work from her editors, she never took any books for granted, putting her all into each and every one.

She spent the afternoon doing laundry and daydreaming about Lloyd and how they seemed to have patched things up in a great way. Who says makeup sex can't move mountains and more?

That notwithstanding, Courtney refused to put too much into their intimacy, deeply passionate as it was. The last time she'd gotten carried away with Lloyd, as though he were hers alone, it had nearly backfired when Courtney hadn't been able to deal with it, allowing herself to act like an insecure woman. Which she wasn't.

Or was she that type and just learning more about herself? She preferred to think otherwise and would not regard Lloyd as if he were her husband. Not yet, anyway.

Courtney was folding clothes when the phone rang. She got to it before her voice mail picked up.

"You're getting harder to reach all the time," her mother complained.

Courtney had been meaning to call her. "I've been really busy."

"Who hasn't? You can always find a few minutes here and there for your mother. You never know how long I'll be around."

Courtney frowned. The guilt trip. She'd heard it all before, but her mother was usually successful.

"Is everything all right?" She recalled her mother's recent cold. Had that been a prelude to something far worse?

"I'm fine. Just wanted to talk to you about the Thanksgiving day meal. Does Lloyd prefer ham or turkey?"

Courtney breathed a sigh of relief, smiling. In fact, she couldn't say which he liked best. She was glad she and Lloyd were back on track and assumed he would still be going with her for Thanksgiving.

"I'm sure either one will work," she said, still learning the types of food that satisfied Lloyd's taste buds.

Dottie sighed. "Well, should we go with sweet potato or apple pie?"

Courtney had never known Dottie to go out of her way to try to impress anyone with meals, which usually stood on their own merits. Why start now?

She decided it was best to try and appease her. "Definitely sweet potato!"

"I was hoping you'd say that. Lester loves my sweet potato pies."

"So did Dad." Courtney had a flash of reminiscence.

"I know. He used to tell me it was the one thing that would always keep him coming back for more."

Courtney gave a little laugh. "You're a great cook, Mom," she reaffirmed. "Lloyd and I are looking forward to spending some time with you and Lester."

"We'll be glad to have you." She paused. "Thank goodness Lloyd caught the person who hit Pilar."

Courtney had left her a voice mail to that effect before going to the cabin. "At least he won't be out there to kill someone else."

"Now you can get on with your own life and Pilar can rest in peace."

Courtney wondered how anyone could rest peacefully after being struck by a drunk driver. As for her own life, it seemed to be headed in the right direction. She would have to see if this proved to be the case over time.

And with Lloyd.

Lloyd sat in his office on Monday morning, reflecting on the weekend he wouldn't soon forget. Courtney had reignited passions that made him happy to be a man—her man—to do with as she pleased. Just as Courtney had allowed herself to have her own sexual impulses satisfied from top to bottom. They certainly seemed to know all the right buttons to push each other to higher limits. He could only imagine how far they could go in establishing something that challenged them even more.

"A penny for your thoughts...."

Lloyd looked up and saw June standing in the doorway. "Hey, there. Was just pondering where we are in the investigation—"

"Seems to me, judging by the smile on your face, you were enjoying more-personal reverie in that head of yours."

He grinned self-consciously. "So you're a mind reader now, among your many talents?"

"I have been told that." She stepped inside the office. "I take it all is well now between you and Courtney?"

"We're getting there," he told her. "Thanks for your advice. It helped."

"That's good to know. Sometimes it's the little things that make a big difference."

"I'll remember that."

"Speaking of which, I'm on the committee for our annual year-end food drive, and we could always use more volunteers. Interested?"

Lloyd nodded. "Sure. Count me in."

She smiled. "Consider yourself counted."

He put that down as yet one more thing to occupy himself with in the foreseeable future, including spending time with Courtney's folks. All part of his new life in Lake Barri. The best of that had proven to be Courtney herself and their growing relationship.

"I've been recruited to help with the department's annual holiday program to collect food for the needy," Lloyd told Courtney that evening.

"Oh, really...?" She glanced up at him. They were in her bed, having just made love.

"Yeah. I'm all for doing my part to help those of lesser means."

"How noble of you." Courtney's leg was draped across

his. The scent of their sex was still in the air, keeping her aroused. "I'd love to help out any way I can."

Lloyd kissed her shoulder. "Are you sure about that? No telling what assignment June might give you, taking away from your writing time."

"I'm sure I can find the time for something so worthy." She loved the feel of his lips on any part of her body. "Besides, it wouldn't be the first thing of this kind I've participated in. Writers are always being asked to lend their name, talents and even money to causes they care about."

He kissed her neck. "In that case, I'll let June know. She'll be happy to have you on board." And it would give them another reason to spend time together.

"Mom's excited about our visit for Thanksgiving," Courtney threw out, trying to ignore the tingly feeling of his kiss now directed at her earlobes.

"So am I. Haven't had a good Thanksgiving meal in a while. Being with family will make it even more special."

Courtney liked how he used the word *family*. Maybe in time her family could become his.

"Hope you like sweet potato pie?"

"Love it! My mother used to buy sweet potato pies from the bakery and I could never get enough."

Courtney smiled at the thought. Their mothers obviously had something in common, to go with their children who were wildly attracted to each other.

She pulled away from Lloyd's wandering hands and

lips, gazing into his eyes. "So if you could be anything other than a police detective, what would it be?"

Lloyd eyed her breasts, perfectly rounded and high, the nipples still erect from his tongue teasing them.

"That's easy. I'd want to be your sex slave, servicing your needs 24/7."

Courtney laughed, feeling a prickle between her legs. "How selfless of you."

"Hey, you asked."

"Better be glad you're still gainfully employed. Otherwise you just might not know a moment's rest, mister."

"I think I could handle it."

"You would say that."

He touched one of her breasts. "We could always put that theory to the test."

She ran a hand up his thigh. "Something tells me we'd both pass with flying colors."

"I was thinking the same thing."

Courtney couldn't stand it any longer and went for his lips, welcoming this playful sexuality between them and what came next. The kiss began as nibbling around the outer edges of Lloyd's mouth before Courtney went for the gusto, sucking on his lower then upper lip, and both at once. She put her tongue inside his mouth and Lloyd took the lead, tasting and sucking it. They gave themselves to each other again with passionate intimacy.

Both were utterly and acutely aware of the other in every respect. Lloyd reveled in Courtney's tender touch as well as giving her every part of himself that she wanted.

Like a runaway freight train, neither could possibly change the direction they were headed, blissfully blazing a path to ultimate fulfillment.

Chapter 24

Dottie and Lester Hartford lived in a condominium complex in Boca Raton overlooking a pond with ducks and geese. The two greeted Courtney and Lloyd as they stepped onto the screened-in porch.

"You made it," Dottie said, hugging her daughter.

"All in one piece." Courtney kissed her cheek.

"Good to see you again, Lloyd." Dottie gave him a quick embrace.

"You, too."

"This is my stepdad, Lester," Courtney told Lloyd after she hugged him.

Lloyd shook his hand, regarding the taller, thinner man with slicked back gray hair. "Nice to meet you."

"Been hearing a lot about you, Lloyd," Lester said.

"I swear none of it is true." Lloyd laughed, hoping the joke wouldn't end up on him.

"Never believed a word of it." Courtney's stepfather offered a crooked smile, seeming to catch on quickly.

"Let's go inside," Dottie said.

Courtney had forgotten just how bright everything was, as though she were in heaven. Even the off-white carpet almost looked as if it had never been walked on. She noted a number of new porcelain dolls her mother had added to the collection since Courtney's last visit, adding to the angelic atmosphere.

Courtney couldn't help but wonder if her mother was somehow trying to make the transition from earth to heaven as easy as possible, though she was still a relatively young woman in her early sixties.

Dottie stopped in the hallway, turning to Courtney. "Here's your room."

Courtney stepped inside the room she assumed she would share with Lloyd. It was in the back of the condo and attractively furnished with a four-poster bed and wardrobe armoire. She sat her bag down on a Turkish area rug.

"Thanks, Mom."

"Lester will show Lloyd his room."

"Excuse me?" Courtney batted her eyes.

"You heard me."

"Mom—"

"Lloyd is more than welcome to our home. I know

you're both grown and sweet on each other. You're not married, though—yet. Call me old-fashioned but…"

"It's cool," Lloyd said, forcing a grin. He would certainly have preferred to share a bed with Courtney, but had to respect her mother's wishes, if only to keep the peace. He said to Lester, "Lead the way…."

Courtney wanted to take a stand. After all, it was her mother who'd invited Lloyd. Was it really necessary to keep them apart even if they weren't married? Since Lloyd had seemed to handle it so graciously, she decided it was better not to make waves.

No one says we can't sneak around a little.

"There you are," Lester said in the guest room.

Lloyd looked around. It was smaller than the other one but clean with a sofa bed opened and made up. "This will be just fine."

"Good. If it were up to me, you two could've stayed in the same room, no problem."

"Don't even give it a second thought." Lloyd was glad to hear that, anyway.

Lester's eyes crinkled. "Can I get you a beer? We also have scotch and wine, as well as good old-fashioned lemonade if you prefer that."

"Beer sounds great."

He followed him to the kitchen, where Lester grabbed two bottles from the refrigerator, tossing one to Lloyd.

"So Dottie tells me you dated Pilar first?"

Oh no, not that again. "I knew Pilar before Courtney and we hung out a couple of times as friends, but that was it."

Lester digested that as he took a swig of beer. "You were the one investigating the hit-and-run?"

"Yes, sir."

"Thanks for doing a good job in apprehending the driver. I never got to know Pilar very well, but Dottie loved her niece like a daughter."

"I'm glad for everyone concerned that we could successfully put this case behind us." Especially Courtney.

Lester scratched his chin. "You're from Alaska, right?"

Lloyd nodded. "Anchorage."

"I was in Alaska once."

"Oh, yeah?"

"My brother lived there for a few years. He taught at the University of Alaska Fairbanks."

"Fairbanks has a lot to offer." Lloyd put the bottle to his mouth and thought of the times he'd been there.

"Nice place to visit but too desolate and way too cold for my tastes," Lester said.

Lloyd laughed. "It's definitely not everyone's cup of tea."

Courtney walked in. "What are you two up to?"

"Lloyd and I were just discussing his great home state," said Lester.

"Don't let him get started. He may never stop." She looked up at Lloyd teasingly and gave him a kiss, tasting the beer on his lips. It was good to see the two getting along. If things went right, they might get to see each other more often.

The thought appealed to Courtney, as it would mean that she and Lloyd had become an item and possibly more.

Chapter 25

Courtney helped Dottie prepare the Thanksgiving day meal. It reminded Courtney of a year ago when Pilar helped her do the same. Neither of them would have ever imagined that it would be their last Thanksgiving together.

"Courtney, dear…" Dottie began, in a voice that automatically sent warning bells to Courtney, as if a prelude to unwanted news. "I need to talk to you."

Courtney stopped chopping celery for the dressing. "Should I be sitting down?" All she could think of was that her mother was suffering from some unknown illness. Was that the whole reason for the invitation to come to Florida?

"No, it's nothing like that." Dottie shook her head

as if reading her mind. "I've already spoken to Lester about this—we think you should consider moving to Boca Raton."

"What?" Courtney's eyes popped wide, as if she had misheard. Even then she felt a sigh of relief that it apparently had nothing to do with her mother's health. Or did it?

Dottie did not flinch. "The one thing I could always count on was that you and Pilar were able to look after each other. Now that your cousin's gone, I worry about you being in Lake Barri by yourself."

"But I'm not by myself, Mom. I have friends there, including Lloyd…"

Dottie sighed while pouring filling into her pie crusts. "I know that, but they're not family."

"Is there something you want to tell me about your health?"

"I'm perfectly fine, child. My knee still bothers me from time to time, but I'm getting used to it. This isn't about me. I just thought it sounded like a good idea. If you don't agree, my feelings won't be hurt."

Courtney gazed at her. "Are you suggesting I move in with you and Lester?"

"Well, you could—just till you found your own place. There's plenty of room here."

Not nearly enough as far as Courtney was concerned. "I'm way too old to move back in with my parents, even for a little while," she said. "Besides, I love my home and living in Lake Barri, wintry weather and all."

"Then that's where you should stay," Dottie said tersely.

"You could always move back home yourself." Courtney wasn't entirely thrilled with the prospect of her mother micromanaging her life at close proximity. But she could deal with it if she had to.

Dottie wiped her hands with a cloth. "Lester and I have made a home here. I'd never want to go back there, other than to visit."

"I understand. I hope you do, too."

Her mother's eyes crinkled. "Of course. You're just like your daddy. Once your mind is made up on something, that's it."

Courtney laughed. "Sounds to me more like I inherited that trait straight from you."

"No comment there." Dottie made a face. "Lloyd must really have you hooked."

It was hard to deny, so Courtney didn't. "How did you guess?"

"It's written all over your face. Haven't seen that certain glow since Joseph died."

"You haven't?" Courtney hadn't meant for it to be so transparent.

"No."

"If that was the case, why would you want me to leave behind someone who means so much to me?"

Dottie smiled. "I don't, dear. Yes, Lester and I talked about you moving here, but I honestly never expected you would go for it. Now I see a big reason why. It's about time you found someone who could make you happy again."

"He does." Courtney bit off a piece of celery, surprised at her mother's astuteness. "There's just something about Lloyd that really feels right."

"Do you love him?" Dottie regarded her.

Courtney considered the question. She wasn't sure of the answer. Lloyd made her feel beautiful, feminine and sexy. Even appreciated and self-assured, by and large. She liked being in his company.

But love? Had it gone that far?

Does Lloyd love me? Or is he holding back for some reason?

"I don't really know what it is I feel," Courtney responded with a catch to her voice. "The relationship has kind of left me in a haze. I'm still sorting out my feelings."

"Well just be careful. The heart can only take so much."

Courtney took heed in the words, having been there. Only, she feared her heart was already too far involved now to pull back anytime soon.

After dinner that evening Courtney and Lloyd took a barefoot stroll on the beach.

Courtney was still thinking about the conversation with her mother. She wondered exactly where things stood between her and Lloyd. Were they really headed to a place where each would get everything wanted out of the relationship?

"Can you believe my mother asked me to move down here?" Courtney said, wanting to gauge his reaction.

"Really?" Lloyd tightened the grip he had on her hand.

"With my mother you can never tell where she's coming from. I don't think she was really all that serious."

But what if she were? He pondered the thought of Courtney moving to Florida, just as he was settling into his job with the Lake Barri Police Department. Where would that leave them?

"So what did you tell her…?"

Courtney could feel his eyes boring into her. She turned to face him. "I told her thanks but no thanks. Does that meet with your approval?"

"I think you know it does."

"Do you think you'll ever want to move back to Alaska?"

Lloyd put his arm around her. Was that a general question? Or one that had a direct impact on their relationship?

"Why, are you looking to take up residence in The Last Frontier state?"

She chuckled softly. "Hardly. It's a bit too frosty up there for me."

Even so, Courtney imagined that the two of them together would warm things up in a hurry.

Lloyd's eyes lowered. "So what's this all about?" He smiled. "Are you trying to get rid of me?"

She laughed. "Not a chance. I just wondered if you might get homesick one day. I'm sure I would."

"I suppose a part of me will always miss Alaska," he conceded. "But life is about accepting new challenges, wherever they may take you. There's really nothing left there for me. You never know, though. If the circumstances were to change, I could end up back where I started."

Courtney assumed he was referring to both his professional and personal circumstances. Such as Lloyd losing his job. Or if their relationship should falter.

The thought of Lloyd leaving Lake Barri caused Courtney's heart to ache. Especially if there was anything she could do to keep him there.

Unless, of course, he wanted to take her with him. At this point, she wouldn't rule anything out when it came to the power of romance and finding one's soul mate.

Chapter 26

On Monday morning Lloyd was back at work on his current case, but Courtney was never far from his thoughts, nor was how much he enjoyed her company. He could see them making their relationship a permanent thing and spending more time in Florida with her mother and stepfather, along with traveling to Lloyd's home state to visit his friends and show off Courtney.

Marriage came to mind as something that seemed like a perfect fit for him and Courtney.

Am I really thinking about walking down the aisle? Is Courtney ready to become a wife again? Could I possibly become the husband and dad my father never was?

Lloyd sat on that thought while taking a phone call.

* * *

"Hello there," Courtney said pleasantly, hoping she wasn't catching Lloyd in the middle of something.

"Hello back."

"I'm at the library and was taking a break."

"Glad you decided to take it with me," he said with enthusiasm.

"You're not busy?"

"Never so busy that I can't make time for a wonderful lady I happen to adore."

She grew warm. "That's so sweet."

"It's also true."

"You know I feel the same way."

Lloyd did, but was happy to hear her verify it, nonetheless. "Guess that makes us the perfect couple."

"I love when you get romantically philosophical."

He laughed. "Would you rather I talked about trying to nab offenders?"

"No, not really."

"Didn't think so."

Courtney was standing between the rows of books. "Do you want to go out for dinner tonight?"

"I'd really love to, but I'll probably be tied up here till late." He didn't want her to ever think it was all about his job and she was second fiddle. "Tomorrow might work, though."

Courtney was beginning to understand that dating a police detective meant being flexible and not expecting everything to go her way. She was up to the challenge.

"All right—let's try for then."

"Great."

"I'd better go. Talk to you later."

"Count on it." Lloyd paused before saying what he felt from the bottom of his heart. "Love you."

The words rang in Courtney's head as she checked out several books. *Love you.* It was something she'd longed to hear again from a man. Especially one with whom her own emotional pull had become so strong. She'd honestly thought that after Joseph another person might never come along to make her feel so wanted, excited and alive.

Lloyd had changed all that. She could only imagine what this man could do for her were they to spend the rest of their lives together.

In her car Courtney headed home while listening to the soulful sounds of Joss Stone.

She pictured Lloyd saying he loved her face-to-face. Could a proposal be that far behind? Or might he get cold feet when it came to taking that next step. After all, he was a lifelong bachelor.

Nor would it be any easier for her, going from widow to matrimony. Courtney had become used to her independence and personal space. Living together as husband and wife would definitely test her mettle.

Somehow, though, Courtney felt she was more than willing to jump the broom if the right offer came along. And Lloyd Vance was just the person to possibly make that offer.

After making a left at the light, Courtney drove down the boulevard till she came to her street.

Standing in the driveway next to an Acura SUV was Olivia. Courtney had completely forgotten that they had an appointment to discuss the characters and illustrations for their next book.

Chapter 27

"I think I'm in love." Courtney steadied the teacup in her hand as they sat in the dining room.

"Oh, really...?" Olivia's mouth hung open as if for effect.

"Yes, really." Courtney had decided to share this news with her best friend before she told Lloyd. Even then, she was hesitant to give that part of herself to Lloyd till she was certain the feelings would be returned in full.

"You think or know...?"

Courtney looked at her squarely. "Okay, I know, and have probably felt this way for some time."

Olivia's eyes lit. "Well you go, girl."

"I intend to." Courtney grew dreamy. "Hopefully to the end of the earth and back with Lloyd."

"I take it he feels the same way?"

"Of course." She again remembered his declaration. "That's what often happens when two people connect in a most amazing way."

"You're right, and I couldn't be happier for you both." Olivia sipped her tea. "Haven't quite reached that stage yet with Jeremy. We're just taking it one step at a time now to see where things go."

"I'm keeping my fingers crossed that it works out for you, too."

"I appreciate that. If it's meant to be…" Olivia gave a thoughtful look, then broke into a smile. "Anyway, right now you're the fortunate one."

"I know. I'm also scared to death about this."

"What's to be scared about?"

"What's not to be? Love opens your heart to anything that can hurt it."

"You mean like other women taking liberties with your man on the dance floor?"

Courtney gave a little laugh. "That's water under the bridge. Besides, we weren't in love then. I doubt Lloyd will want to do any more dirty dancing with someone else when I'll be there to give him all he can handle."

"Then, what?"

"Well, with Lloyd being a cop, it's scary not knowing from day to day if he'll be hurt. Or worse. After Joseph and then Pilar, I just don't know if I could handle it if something bad happened to Lloyd."

"You can't look at it that way," Olivia insisted. "There are no guarantees in life. Who says that you or I won't run into harm's way at a book signing? Home invasion? Or even just going to the store? Point is, we have to live for today. What happens tomorrow it out of our hands."

"Is it really?"

"Yes, but that doesn't mean you shouldn't plan for tomorrow and many days, months and years after. You deserve to be happy and so does Lloyd. Just relax, stop worrying and let it happen."

Courtney couldn't help but smile. "It's nice to have such a positive presence in my life."

"Wouldn't have it any other way." Olivia gazed across the table. "So with love in the air, it shouldn't be long before Lloyd pops the question."

Courtney batted her eyes. "Aren't you jumping the gun just a bit? Who said anything about marriage?"

"Well, excuse me for being presumptuous, but you're allowed to remarry. And don't tell me you'd be happy being in love without a ring on your finger to make it official."

Courtney sat back. The truth was, she was ready to tie the knot again with someone she loved. But only if he felt the same. Was Lloyd at least thinking about it?

"Of course I'd love to get married again," she conceded. "I just don't want to get my hopes up, only to be let down."

"I hear you." Olivia grabbed a coconut bar from the plate. "So I guess the ball's in Lloyd's court. And I think he'll send it back your way in no time flat."

Courtney wasn't so sure about that, given that Lloyd must have been in love before. Yet he had still never even become engaged as far as she knew. Was that more about the previous women in Lloyd's life? Or him?

"It would be great to see you as a mother." Olivia wiped crumbs from her lips. "Which means I'd be a godmother."

Courtney half grinned. "Now you're really getting carried away. Before you have me married, pregnant and barefoot, why don't we just wait to see where Lloyd stands on all this."

"Fair enough."

Courtney reached for a coconut bar. Not to say that she wouldn't love to be the mother of Lloyd's children. But that wasn't something Courtney could decide on her own. He would certainly have some say in the matter.

In any event, it took time and planning before she would consider bringing a child or children into this world. It was obvious Lloyd felt the same way, given how serious he was about using protection every time they had sex.

She wondered how much of that had to do with

being abandoned by his father. Did Lloyd think he was somehow biologically predisposed to being a bad parent?

Courtney tasted her tea, putting those thoughts aside. Right now she only wanted to enjoy the idea of being in love and having it returned. Everything else would very likely take care of itself.

Chapter 28

The following night, Courtney and Lloyd had dinner at a jazz supper club and then went back to Lloyd's house, where they stripped naked and made love.

Courtney clung to Lloyd as his erection impaled her time and time again, bringing her each time to the edge of orgasm before pulling back, causing slow and exquisite torture.

They kissed lustfully, their mouths open, their bodies gleaming and spirits in tune. When time came for the moment of climax, Courtney absorbed Lloyd's powerful thrusts, constricting tightly around him, wanting to never let go.

Lloyd grunted loudly as his release came, while

Courtney's own sounds were softer but coming from the same satisfaction.

"I enjoyed dessert even more than dinner tonight," he whispered against her ear afterward.

"So did I." Courtney's heart was still beating fast, still coming down from the high. Her desire for Lloyd seemed to grow each time they were together. She couldn't help but wonder if that was a recipe for a fall.

Lloyd kissed her head. "You're really something else."

She untangled herself and ran a finger across his nipple, eyeing him. "You said you love me. Did you mean it?"

Lloyd held her gaze and put his heart out there, realizing there was no turning back from this point on. "Every last word and a few more."

"Such as...?"

"Such as you have my *complete* and undivided attention where it concerns women."

Courtney smiled, music to her ears. "I love you, too," she said.

Lloyd returned the smile. "I was hoping to hear those words come from your lips."

"Now you have."

"Say it again."

She colored. "I love you, Lloyd Vance."

He beamed. "I love you, too, Courtney Hudson."

Courtney allowed herself a moment to savor the pronouncement. She made a murmuring sound.

Lloyd kissed her. "We're good for each other."

"I know." She licked her lips.

"I'd never do anything to intentionally hurt you."

"I believe that, too."

He touched her thigh. "The moment I first laid eyes on you, I knew there was something between us."

She stretched her leg across his. "So you're a psychic?" And a very sexy one at that.

"Not exactly. But my instincts are usually right on the money."

"In that case, you should definitely trust your instincts."

Lloyd slid his hand down between her legs. "Oh, I fully intend to."

Courtney felt the embers burning deep inside with his touch. She reached up to taste his lips again. They were taking things to a new level in this relationship, and she was more than ready for the journey, wherever it may lead them.

The annual year-end holiday food drive was well underway. Lloyd expected Courtney to walk in at any moment. He was happy she had volunteered her services. It told him that she not only wanted to be his woman in a very private way, but also involved in his life and obligations as a cop. Just as he would like nothing better than to be there to support her writing career any way he could.

"You all right there, Vance?" June touched his arm.

"I'm fine. Just slightly overwhelmed."

A large warehouse had been donated for the food drive and it appeared they would need every inch of it to accommodate what people were contributing. Lloyd shoved a cart of canned food toward a table.

She chuckled. "Thought you would have known by now just how generous the people of Lake Barri could be, especially at this time of year."

"I'm beginning to appreciate it all the more."

"Heard you arrested a man for the murder of Jasmine Johnston?"

"Yeah, got a match on a print and DNA." Furrows lined Lloyd's forehead. "Unfortunately the 'man' is just a teenager, who apparently was still bitter after the victim dumped him. Blake Ramsey followed her to the lake where they scuffled before he killed her."

June wrinkled her nose. "Such a waste of two lives."

"Tell me about it. Meth, volatile relationships and wayward youth can sure make a lethal combination."

"True. Too bad we can usually only intervene once the damage has been done."

"You certainly won't have to hit the streets much longer." Lloyd observed her bulging stomach.

June glanced him sideways. "I'm looking forward to maternity leave, to tell you the truth. My husband can't wait till we give birth."

"Motherhood suits you."

"That's what my own mother tells me. At the same time, she keeps saying it will be the hardest thing I ever do."

Lloyd nodded, remembering his mother's struggles to raise him and keep food on the table.

"I'm sure she's right." He looked over her head toward the entrance, a smile tugging at his lips. "There's Courtney."

Carrying a box of nonperishable food items, Courtney stepped into the warehouse. The place was busy with people coming in and out and volunteers in various stages of work. She wished now that she had done her part in previous years with the police department's food drive. Never too late, though, to lend a helping hand to those in need.

She spotted Lloyd coming her way with a pregnant woman.

"Glad you could make it," Lloyd said.

"Wouldn't have had it any other way."

He kissed her. "Let me take that for you."

"Thanks." Courtney handed him the box.

"You must be Courtney. The lady Lloyd has kept all to himself and can't stop talking about."

Courtney smiled. "And you must be June."

She nodded. "Looks like Lloyd's been talking about both of us. We're happy to have you."

"I'm ready to roll up my sleeves and get to work," Courtney declared.

"A person after my own heart," June said to Lloyd. "Hope you don't mind if I steal your girlfriend?"

"Be my guest. I've got to get back to my own station." He met Courtney's eyes. "I'll catch up with you later."

"Bye."

She gave a little wave and prepared herself for whatever they wanted her to do. Courtney could see that it wouldn't be long before June gave birth.

As though reading her mind, June said, "If everything goes right, our baby should enter this world on March fifteenth."

"How nice. Is this your first?"

"Yeah, but probably not the last, if my husband has his wish."

Courtney laughed. She wondered if it was Lloyd's dream to have a houseful of kids. Or would he settle for one or two?

"Do you have any kids?" June asked as they headed toward a row of tables.

"Not yet." She'd love to become a mother, if it was God's plan. And if the timing worked out for her and her partner.

"I should've guessed, with that beautiful figure you have."

Courtney wondered how she could tell what kind of figure she had under the wide-leg pants and baggy sweater.

"I'll be happy to lose it for a little while if things work out that way."

"Something tells me Lloyd would welcome your attitude, assuming you two are headed in that direction…."

"Maybe down the line." Courtney was willing to put that out there knowing Lloyd as she had come to. But children would have to wait. She wasn't interested in having kids out of wedlock and couldn't imagine Lloyd would want that, either.

They came to a table and were greeted by a petite, white-haired woman.

"Emma, this is Courtney," June said. "Why don't you have her sort items into bins or relabel boxes."

"Okay." Emma smiled, adjusting her glasses.

"Thanks." June looked at Courtney. "If you need anything, just holler."

"Got it."

Courtney watched her walk away. She was already beginning to feel like she was part of Lloyd's professional world, and welcomed another way to give back to the community. It seemed as if their lives were converging in the most wonderful of ways, which boded well for the future.

Chapter 29

With the New Year just minutes away, Courtney had a quiet moment of reflection while Lloyd opened a bottle of champagne. She had lost her cousin and found love in less than three months. Now she was about to enter another phase of life with all the hope and promise it held. In spite of her fear of the unknown, Courtney embraced the future and the prospect of spending it with Lloyd.

As the countdown began, Lloyd hoisted his champagne flute. "Here's to a brand-new year filled with happiness, enrichment and endless possibilities...."

Courtney tapped her glass against his. "And here's to you, Lloyd, for being such a wonderful guy."

"I'll drink to that." He flashed a wide smile and tasted the champagne. "And to the fact that I just happen to be with the most beautiful, sexiest woman I've ever known."

"Oh…" she cooed and sipped the drink before lifting her face to kiss him.

Lloyd put his arm around her waist, pulling them closer, and tilted Courtney back before resuming the kiss. He couldn't help but think that their journey had only just begun. There was no one he desired to be with more. Or could imagine making a life with.

Courtney felt as if she were floating on air while Lloyd held her, his mouth pressed down firmly on hers. She wrapped an arm tightly around his neck and took in the kiss while giving back with equal fervor. Their tongues met, and Courtney felt a little light-headed as she lost herself in love.

"Happy New Year, Courtney," Lloyd said jubilantly.

"Happy New Year to you, too, sweetheart." It was the first time she had used this endearment with him, and Courtney realized it came naturally, as if he had always been that to her.

Courtney wasn't sure how long the kiss lasted. Only that it seemed to go on forever and she had absolutely no problem with that.

The courtroom was deathly quiet as the defendant rose to make a statement prior to formal sentencing. Gordon McNair, wearing a gray suit, stared straight ahead.

Courtney noted that his entire family was seated

behind him in the gallery. She felt for them as she would any family that had to deal with the fallout of a hit-and-run fatality. But her sorrow was more for the tremendous loss of Pilar, who Courtney still couldn't believe was gone forever.

She sat next to Lloyd and June behind the prosecutor's table.

Courtney glanced at Lloyd. His jawline was tense with anticipation. He turned her way and his eyes crinkled as they held hands.

Lloyd was glad this was the final stage of the case against Gordon McNair, who had plea bargained to get a reduced sentence for hitting Pilar with his BMW and fleeing the scene, leaving her for dead. While Pilar would never know the long and full life she deserved because of a drunk driver, Lloyd wanted to believe she would be satisfied that justice had been served.

It would allow him and Courtney to put this tragedy behind them once and for all and concentrate on their own future. One that Pilar would surely have been a big part of had misfortune not struck.

Lloyd eyed the defendant.

McNair pointed a contrite gaze in Courtney's direction for a long moment, before speaking in an uneven voice. "I would like to say to the court and, in particular, to Pilar Kendall's family, I know no words can possibly atone for what I've done. I will have to live the rest of my life knowing that I alone was responsible for ending the life of someone I knew and respected as a fellow teacher. I betrayed not only Pilar, but my own family. I did a stupid thing out of fear, ignorance and cowardice—and now I'm paying the price. I'm so sorry for all the pain I've caused. Please forgive me—"

Courtney felt tears sting her cheeks. She wasn't sure how much of the statement was prepared by the defense for impact and what words, if any, truly came from his heart. Either way, she felt that something good had come out of this—acknowledged guilt and time spent in prison to atone. She also hoped it put the spotlight on the terrible consequences of driving under the influence and failing to stop when involved in a traffic accident.

Her grip tightened around Lloyd's hand, and Courtney watched as the judge pronounced his sentence.

Chapter 30

It was nearly midnight when Lloyd was startled awake by the phone. He uncoiled himself from Courtney's warm body and grabbed his cell phone.

"Mr. Vance, this is Sheryl Glade of the Murray Hills Nursing Home. I'm calling to inform you that Mimi Redgrave passed away in her sleep this evening. You were on her contact list."

"Thanks for telling me." Lloyd's voice thickened. "Do you know when the funeral will be?"

She put him on hold. A minute later he had his answer.

Courtney awakened, having fallen into a deep sleep after making love. She could tell by the gist of Lloyd's words that someone he knew had died. When he hung up, she waited tensely to learn who the person was.

"My great-aunt Mimi died," he informed her.

Courtney cocked a brow. "You never told me about her."

"I haven't seen her much in recent years. After my mother's death, she picked up the slack somewhat and helped me deal with it. Auntie Mimi, as I called her, was in her late eighties. She's been out of it for a while, suffering from Alzheimer's and diabetes. So it isn't a really big surprise that she's dead, but it's sad nonetheless."

"Are you going to her funeral?"

Lloyd was hesitant to do so, given the fact that he was busy at work and wasn't eager to be away from Courtney for even a short while. But since Aunt Mimi had been the closest thing to a parent his mother had known, it seemed like the right thing to do.

"I think I will."

"Can I go with you?"

He faced her in the soft light. "Would you?"

"I'd be happy to." Courtney touched his face. "I want to be there to share your joy and pain. And it would be nice to see some of Alaska, too."

Lloyd kissed her hand. "I'd love to take you home."

They arrived at the Ted Stevens Anchorage International Airport. After renting a car, Lloyd gave Courtney an abbreviated tour of the city, pointing out the Alaska

Native Heritage Center, Town Square Park, Museum of History and Fine Art, and University of Alaska Anchorage.

"Nice." Courtney soaked it all in, amazed that she was actually in Alaska, albeit for a somber occasion. At least Lloyd's great-aunt had lived a full life, something that Pilar and Joseph had been deprived of.

"It's even better in the summer." Lloyd peeked at the digital temperature gauge in car, which read twenty-one degrees. "There's a lot more I can show you."

"I'd love it!" Courtney could imagine visiting Anchorage a couple of times a year, acquainting herself with the culture and world where Lloyd grew up.

He was hoping she would say that. Suddenly Lloyd embraced the idea of returning to Alaska to vacation periodically. At one time he couldn't get out of the state fast enough, disillusioned over one thing or another. But things had changed with Courtney in his life. He wanted her to experience the best that Anchorage had to offer. Rather than run from his past, Lloyd now saw it as something that could work in his favor.

They checked into a hotel and freshened up.

Lloyd drew Courtney near, his nose picking up the floral fragrance of her perfume, enticing him. "Maybe we should just stay here for a while…"

Courtney glanced at the king-size bed and was more than a little tempted to make good use of it now. But there would be time for that later.

She gazed up at Lloyd, feeling the warmth emanating

from his body. "Hold on to those naughty thoughts. We really should pay our respects to your auntie Mimi first."

"Do we have to?" Lloyd frowned, feeling an urge building inside to have her on the spot.

"Yes!" Courtney kissed his lips, and then used her pinkie to wipe raspberry lip gloss from them.

He half grinned, knowing she was right. They had the better part of two full days for intimacy.

"You win. Let's go."

Lloyd and Courtney walked up a hill before entering the Mountain Vista Funeral Home. As they approached the casket, Lloyd felt a little guilty that he hadn't kept in touch with the woman who, in many ways, had acted as a substitute mother.

Mimi Redgrave looked like she was sleeping peacefully. Her pale, weathered features were surrounded by snow-white hair, and a simple dark dress was loose on her frail frame.

"Excuse me…?" a voice said from behind.

Lloyd turned and saw a middle-aged female. "Hi."

"I'm Sheryl Glade from the nursing home."

"Lloyd Vance, and this is Courtney Hudson."

"Nice to meet you both." Her eyes focused on Lloyd. "Thanks for coming. I'm sure Mimi would've been happy to know you came."

"I wanted to do right by Auntie Mimi," he said solemnly.

"You are."

Lloyd thought of his mother and how much he missed her, just as he would Aunt Mimi. He regarded Courtney, glad to have another strong woman in his life to carry the torch of those who had passed on.

Courtney gazed at Lloyd's great-aunt. The fact that she lived so long was something not many achieved. *I'll bet she could have told me a story or two about Lloyd as a boy*. Courtney held back tears as she faced Lloyd, gently squeezing his hand.

Soon they were mingling with relatives and others who knew Mimi in what turned into a celebration of her long life rather than mourning her death.

Courtney took note of a tall, trim man who came in and seemed fixated on Lloyd. Or was it her imagination?

Perhaps he was an old acquaintance of Mimi's? Or he was someone else who knew the family.

The man suddenly locked eyes with Courtney and began to move. She tapped Lloyd's shoulder, interrupting his conversation with Sheryl.

Lloyd faced Courtney, wondering if the atmosphere was starting to get to her just a little.

"Do you know that gentleman who's coming our way?" she asked evenly.

Lloyd looked up. A sixty-something man in a brown suit stood before them. His face had some age lines and his short hair was now gray and receding, but Lloyd would know him anywhere.

Even though he would rather forget.

"Hello, Lloyd," the man said in a scratchy voice.

Courtney could see the tension in Lloyd's face as he simply stared but said nothing.

"Who is he?" she whispered.

Lloyd stiffened. "My father."

Chapter 31

"What the hell are you doing here?" Lloyd could barely believe his eyes, while straining to control his emotions.

"Came to see you."

Lloyd's nostrils expanded. "It's a bit too late for that."

"Just give me a few minutes—"

"I'm not giving you another second!" Lloyd glared. "Stay away from me."

He stormed away, wanting to get as far away from his father as he could.

Courtney was about to follow when she felt a strong hand on her arm. She turned and stared into the face of the elder Vance.

"Wait," he said. "You're his woman?"

"Yes. Courtney."

"Courtney, talk to him for me, please."

She hesitated. "I'm not sure I can do that. This is between you and—"

"Look, I screwed up. I want to try to make amends now. Will you help me?"

Courtney had little or no desire to help mend fences between son and long-lost father. Mainly because she knew Lloyd wanted no part of the man he blamed for ruining his childhood. But there was such a thing as forgiveness. The man was reaching out to Lloyd—his only living parent. Could she really turn her back on that, realizing she would give anything to have her own father alive again?

Courtney met his gray-brown eyes and waited for him to release her. "What do you want me to do?"

He sighed. "Tell Lloyd I need to talk to him. I'll be at the Wolf Café at nine." He reached into his back pocket. "Here's my card."

Courtney looked at. It identified him as Victor J. Vance, electrical engineer and consultant.

"I'll try, but I can't guarantee that he'll show—"

"Thank you," he broke in. "It's all I can ask. I'll look forward to seeing my son."

Courtney watched him walk away. She glanced at his card again and went to find Lloyd.

Having cooled down a bit, Lloyd was about to head back inside when Courtney came through the door.

"Where were you?" he asked. He had been ready to go back to the hotel as soon as he saw his father.

"Can we talk?" There was a catch in her voice.

Lloyd wasn't sure he liked the sound of that. "Yeah, in the car."

Courtney fastened her seat belt and waited for him to drive off, having second thoughts about getting involved in Lloyd's family politics. Yet if they were going to be together, she had to at least be able to offer her opinion on touchy subjects.

She watched Lloyd's profile as he gazed out over the steering wheel. "Your dad wants you to meet with him tonight."

Lloyd regarded her with austere disapproval. "That what he told you?"

She nodded with a swallow.

"Well, it's not going to happen—not tonight, not ever. I never want to see him again!"

"You have every right to feel that way," she conceded.

Lloyd gripped the steering wheel so hard that his knuckles ached. "After the hell he put my mother through, I'm not about to reward his coming out of the woodwork by pretending he's my father."

Courtney's mouth pursed. "But he is your father."

"In name only. That doesn't give him the right to come back into my life after being a no-show for so many years."

"I agree that there's no good excuse for him abandoning you and your mom. But maybe he just wants to explain what happened. You should at least hear him out."

"Oh, so now you're taking his side?" Lloyd snorted with disbelief.

"Of course not. I just think that since he bothered to show up, it might be a good idea to try and patch things up. Otherwise you might never get another chance and you might regret it for the rest of your life."

Courtney had no desire to make him feel guilty. But she also knew that Lloyd was not thinking clearly when it came to his father. She only wanted to help as someone who loved him and could see things from a different perspective.

Would he listen? Or would this drive a wedge between them?

"I guess I'll just have to take my chances on that," he said sarcastically. "If my father cared about me at all, he would have stayed away and not brought back painful memories."

"That doesn't make sense."

Lloyd's brows descended sharply. "What doesn't make sense is you carrying on a conversation with my father behind my back."

"It wasn't like that," she insisted.

"Sure as hell seems like it to me. I came here to pay respects to my great-aunt, not to allow my father to try and worm his way back into my life by sweet-talking my girlfriend. He's as good as dead as far as I'm concerned. End of story."

Courtney did not try to carry it any further. The last thing she wanted was to see her relationship with Lloyd deteriorate because of the deep issues with his father. She would leave that up to them to work out.

They didn't say another word to each another for rest of the drive back to their hotel.

Lloyd scolded himself as Courtney sat in a chair flipping pages of a magazine. She probably wished they had gotten separate rooms right about now. And he couldn't blame her. He'd acted with his wounded heart and not his head when he struck out at her in lieu of his father.

Yes, there was some definite pent-up anger on his part, and deservedly so, all things considered. But he couldn't let that cloud his judgment, especially where it concerned Courtney. No matter how sour the taste in his mouth.

Not only do I have to hear him say his peace, I need to, if only for some closure…and to try and make amends with Courtney, who was only trying to help and deserved a more mature response from me.

He walked over to her. "So when and where does my father want to meet?"

Courtney lifted her eyes and told him.

"All right. I'll go talk with him, but I can't guarantee it will change things."

She brushed aside a stray hair. "All I ask is that you go with an open mind."

"I'll try," he promised.

"Do you want me to go with you?"

"I think I should do this alone."

She expected as much, standing. "I'll be here when you get back."

"I shouldn't be too long." He connected with her eyes. "Sorry about earlier."

"No need to apologize. You had every right to vent your feelings under the circumstances." Nevertheless, she was happy to see that he had come around to her way of thinking.

Courtney kissed him for luck and with the depth of her feelings for Lloyd.

Lloyd left still thinking about the kiss, as well as the confrontation that lay ahead.

Chapter 32

Lloyd entered the Wolf Café at nine sharp. He didn't want to wait for his father. Or give the man an excuse to bolt before he could take him to task on why he'd abandoned Lloyd and his mother.

He found him seated in a booth sipping coffee.

Victor brightened when he saw Lloyd. "Wasn't sure if you'd come."

"Believe me, I didn't want to. But—"

"Your girlfriend thought you should. She's a pretty one and obviously smart, too."

"This isn't about her," Lloyd stated brusquely.

"True enough." His father indicated the other side of the table. "Sit."

Lloyd obeyed, wondering if this was a big mistake—providing an audience for someone who didn't deserve one. But he had made a commitment to Courtney that he would do so without prejudice, if possible.

"I took the liberty of ordering two black coffees," Victor said. "Hope that's okay with you?"

"That's fine." Lloyd paused, not wanting to get too comfortable. "I don't suppose it would be too much of a stretch to say I never thought I'd see you again. Or that I even wanted to."

"I can understand that."

I doubt it. "Momma hoped you'd come back someday while she was still alive. So did I. Guess you fooled us."

"I made some mistakes." Victor pinched his nose. "Look, I know I have no right to come back into your life now—"

"So why did you?"

"Heard about Mimi's death. Since she was like a grandmother to you, I figured you might show up."

"So you got that right. Hooray. It still doesn't tell me why you're here."

Victor drew a breath. "You're my son. I decided maybe it wasn't too late to have some sort of relationship."

Lloyd couldn't help but chuckle derisively. "You're joking, right? Now, why the hell would I want any type of relationship with you?"

"Because I'm your father," he responded sharply.

"You gave up that right a long, long time ago."

"Whatever you may think, I never stopped caring about you." Victor shook as he sipped coffee. "Things went sour between me and your mother. It had nothing to do with you."

"It had everything to do with me. When you hurt her, you hurt me."

"I'm sorry you feel that way, but things happen between grown folks. I tried to make the marriage work. It just wasn't meant to be."

"So you just left us?" Lloyd's eyes bulged.

"I had no choice. Your mother and I were fighting and arguing over every little thing. Something had to give. Turned out to be me."

"You left us with nothing! Do you expect a pat on the back for that?"

"No, you deserved better and I'm sorry."

Lloyd curled his lip. "That won't cut it."

"It was your mother's choice not to take anything from me. Wasn't for lack of trying. She was too damn proud for her own good." Victor leaned forward. "That doesn't excuse what I did to you and her and I deeply regret it."

"So I'm supposed to feel sorry for you now?"

Victor sighed. "I'd never expect that. But for what it's worth, I sent cards and money to you for years."

"I never received a damn thing from you." Lloyd's jaw clenched, the words empty to him.

"That's because they were always returned unopened. I suppose it was your mother's way of punishing me even more for leaving her."

"You're lying!"

"Now why would I do that? Isn't it a bit late in the game to make up stories that you might not want to hear? It's the truth, son."

Lloyd slowly lifted the coffee mug and took a sip. Could he have been mistaken about him all these years? Had his mother kept that from him as part of her own coping mechanism or bitterness? Or perhaps to protect him?

"Even if I believed you, Momma's been dead for a while now. You certainly made no effort to contact me since."

Victor frowned. "Since there was no indication you wanted to hear from me, I basically gave up trying, figuring you'd find a way to reach me when you were ready." He wiped his mouth. "I moved to the lower forty-eight for a while, there, before resettling in Anchorage last year. Heard you moved to Colorado?"

"Yeah." Lloyd wanted to sulk but found it hard to hate him, even with all that had happened in the past.

"And you're a cop?"

He nodded. "For more than a decade now."

"You happy with the job?"

"Pretty much." Lloyd paused. "I saw your card. Still an engineer, I see."

"Saw no reason to change occupations." Victor grinned. "The world can always use good engineers."

"Did you ever remarry? Have other kids?" Lloyd wondered if he actually had siblings he'd never known.

Victor shook his head. "Never remarried and no other children. Maybe I wasn't cut out to be a family man. Or maybe no one else ever came along to make me get over your mother and you. I don't know."

Lloyd wasn't sure if his father was trying to soften the blow of abandonment or if he realized what he'd given up. Either way, it was still a tough pill to swallow, no matter how much Lloyd wanted to forgive and forget.

The waitress came and warmed up their coffee.

"So is it serious with you and Courtney?" Victor narrowed one eye.

"I'm in love with her."

"Well, I'm happy for you and I hope it works out."

It was a thought Lloyd echoed, not wanting to see their relationship end prematurely like his parents' marriage. Not when he envisioned so much more to look forward to with Courtney.

"Thanks."

Victor studied his coffee before looking at Lloyd. "I know I'm probably asking a lot here, but if you can find it in you, I'd like to stay in touch."

Lloyd observed the man before him. If someone had told him yesterday that he would be having coffee with his father and talking about reconciliation, he would have labeled the person certifiably insane. How could he not have?

Now Lloyd believed it might be time to heal old wounds and hang on to the only family he had left.

"I think I'd like that, too."

* * *

"It's beautiful here," Courtney told her mother over the phone, glancing out the window at the city's lights. "And it's dark, cold and snowy. Not to say that it's all that warm right now in Lake Barri."

"You think you might want to live there?" Dottie asked.

"Probably not. Never say never, though." Courtney liked living in Colorado. But she saw no reason why she couldn't expand her horizons someday to include Alaska if the conditions were right—such as marriage and a husband who grew nostalgic.

"I'd like you to send me an autographed copy of your latest book. My friend's granddaughter is a big fan and she would love it. I'll send you the money."

"Don't be silly. I'll be happy to send the book, Mom."

Dottie mumbled something away from the phone. "So, where's Lloyd?"

Courtney told her about Lloyd's reunion with his father. She hoped they weren't at each other's throats. She didn't want to be blamed for talking Lloyd into the meeting if it went awry.

"I'm sorry Lloyd and his father were estranged for so long."

"Me, too." Courtney tried to imagine what it would have been like if her own parents had been apart during her formative years. How much of a difference would that have made to her life now? Would she have been able to weather the storm as Lloyd had?

"Well, the important thing is that they're talking now," Dottie uttered. "People can change over time."

"You think?"

"Of course. Sometimes it just takes certain events to occur before that happens."

Courtney considered how her mother had gone through changes, first with her father's death and then Pilar's.

I've changed, too, determined to get the most out of life every day and not take anything for granted. Especially the simple things.

Even her relationship with Lloyd was something Courtney wanted to continuously work at to keep strong. No matter what happened between Lloyd and his father tonight.

Courtney had just poured herself a glass of wine and sat down to watch TV when the door opened.

Lloyd came in, his expression unreadable.

"Well…how did it go?" she asked with trepidation.

He paused, staring down at her, before breaking into a grin. "We're going to try and work things out."

"Really?"

"Yeah. I'm not saying the past will be swept under the rug, 'cause that's not happening. Too many bad memories. But I really want to put forth an effort to get to know my old man for the first time in my life."

Courtney stood, her eyes watering with happiness for Lloyd. She hugged him and whispered, "Thank you."

"No, thank you." Lloyd felt his own tears building.

"If you hadn't come with me to Anchorage, I'm not sure that—"

"Shh…" She put a finger to his lips. "Don't even think about the what-if. All that matters is we're together and things seem to be working out right as a result."

"They do indeed." He kissed her soft lips, tasting wine. "My very beautiful good-luck charm."

"That works both ways." She kissed him back, feeling her libido kick into gear. "Why don't we finish this in bed?"

Lloyd shuddered at the thought, needing the release and wanting mutual satisfaction.

"Why don't we?" he murmured in her ear.

They made love lasciviously, experimenting in new, erotic, passionate ways and returning to previous tried and true ones, pleasuring each other to dizzying heights.

Courtney basked in Lloyd's scent and the tenderness of his fingers and mouth exploring her inside and out. In turn, she did her best to ignite him through her kisses, touch and responsiveness.

Their bodies contoured perfectly as the fire between them became an all-out inferno. They came together time and time again with a ravenous appetite that seemed to know no end.

"Lloyd…" Courtney's voice purred as she galloped atop him, feeling his erection hitting the mark over and over again. She arched her back while he massaged her breasts, his magical fingers nimbly caressing and teasing her nipples. "Oh, my darling…it feels so good."

"Back at you, baby." Lloyd loved being beneath Courtney, watching her take control so masterfully.

When his turn came, they reversed positions without breaking stride.

Courtney's nails ran torturously up and down Lloyd's back as she lifted herself to him and he plunged deeper and deeper inside her. His tepid breath on her face intensified with each stroke, while Courtney's own breathing was choppy and her heart seemed like it would explode in the heat of the moment. Her orgasm came with a jolt, ripping through her body with pulsating pleasure.

She waited and watched as Lloyd climaxed, his body shuddering wildly atop her, letting Courtney know how good it was for him, too.

Lloyd enjoyed one final thrust while kissing Courtney's face, her legs spread wide beneath him, body damp from their sex. He sucked in a deep breath and put his mouth on hers. He wanted only to make Courtney happy and give her all he had in that regard.

As the sensations subsided, each had worn the other down to a frazzle. Courtney rested her head on Lloyd's shoulder, wanting only to sleep, content in their togetherness. She felt luxurious in that moment of being in love and loved by another so gentle and giving.

Chapter 33

A month later Courtney was busy at work on her manuscript and looking at another deadline. She had just spoken to her editor, who wanted to get the book out in time for the Christmas holiday season. Courtney expected to do a book tour for this one. She hoped Lloyd would be able to join her at some point along the journey for a little romantic getaway.

The thought of their making love was fresh on her mind from last night. In fact, every time was an adventure in and of itself. Being in love made their sexual compatibility that much more incredible.

The bell rang and Courtney left her musings and laptop for the door.

It was Lloyd, looking sharp in a navy business suit. "Hello, there."

"Well hello, handsome."

He kissed her, loving the citrus scent of Courtney's perfume. But then, what didn't he like about her? This was why Lloyd had come to an important decision about cementing their future.

"What are you up to?"

She rolled her eyes. "Guess?"

He grinned. "Your next bestseller, of course."

"One can only hope. Never gets any easier with all the competition."

"That's what motivates you to be as good as you are."

"I suppose." Courtney scratched her nose. "Can I get you something to drink?"

"Actually I can't stay long. I just came by for something…"

"Not *that* something?"

He laughed, still basking in their last marathon performance. "No, not that."

Lloyd was acting strange. What was going on?

She stared at his face. "Please don't keep me in suspense. What's up?"

He smiled and took her hand, leading her to the living room. *I didn't realize I'd be this nervous—and excited at the same time.*

Lloyd gazed down into Courtney's eyes. "Will you marry me?"

Her mouth hung open, as if she'd misheard him. Though, in fact, she had heard him quite clearly.

"Are you serious?"

"I've never been more." His voice was steady. "I love you, darling. We're practically married right now with all the time we spend together. I want to make it official as man and wife."

This was something Courtney wanted, too, from the depths of her heart. She loved Lloyd to death and was certain they could have a long, happy marriage with all the trimmings.

"Yes, yes, yes, I'll marry you!" She wanted to shout it to the rooftops. "I love you, Lloyd, and would like nothing better than to be your blushing bride forever and a day!"

He flashed a brilliant smile and gave her a long, deep kiss. "You've made me the happiest man."

Courtney tasted his lips, trying to keep from crying. "I'm glad, because you've made me the happiest woman in the world."

"We can go big or small as far as the wedding is concerned. I'll leave that up to you."

"Bigger than big!" she told him excitedly, recalling that her first wedding was very small and simple. "I want everyone we know to be there and share our special moment with us."

"Then so be it. Whatever you want."

Courtney brushed tears from her cheeks. "I have everything I want right in front of me."

"So do I." Lloyd kissed her again. "One more thing…" He took a ring out of his pocket. "It belonged to my mother. She wanted me to give it to the woman I asked to marry."

He slid it on Courtney's finger, fearful it might not fit.

But the ring went on easily, and Courtney held her hand up in the air. "Perfect," she declared, tears streaming down her face.

"No, you're perfect." Lloyd hugged her, feeling Courtney's arms wrap around his neck.

"We're the perfect couple!"

"Can't argue with that." He leaned back and smiled at her. "Not one bit."

"Neither can I." She kissed him again and again and could only imagine the joy and blessings that surely awaited them.

Epilogue

It was a perfect day for a wedding, with blues skies and lots of sunshine. A light breeze came in off the lake, keeping temperatures pleasant. The guests were up on their feet as a string quartet began to play Beethoven's "Ode to Joy."

Lloyd was nervous as he stood in a designer tuxedo awaiting his bride to be. This was his true love, the woman he had hoped to find and commit to for the rest of his life. Courtney had proven to be that woman in all she stood for. She was about to make him the happiest man on the planet. And in a few months they would add to the joy when their offspring came into their world, reflecting what true family was all about.

Lloyd glanced at his father, seated next to Courtney's mother. The two men shared a moment of mutual respect before Lloyd eyed June next to her husband. He was holding their son, Eduardo. Lloyd looked at the maid of honor, Olivia, and then turned to his best man, Steven, who offered a comforting smile.

Finally Lloyd's gaze moved to the arch in the row of rosebushes from which Courtney would soon emerge with her stepfather.

Riveted, Lloyd sucked in a deep breath as Courtney started to walk down the aisle.

Courtney endeavored to keep tears from smearing her makeup. She wasn't sure if that was possible, given the sheer ecstasy she felt in soon becoming Mrs. Lloyd Vance. She glowed radiantly as she thought about the life they'd created now growing inside her.

She kept her chin up and shoes straight while moving gracefully in an ivory sleeveless wedding dress with a scoop neckline and lace bodice. Her hair was in a loose updo, and Courtney relished the occasion to be at her most beautiful for the handsome man she would wed.

When she arrived at his side, Courtney could only beam with love and longing. She saw the glow in Lloyd's eyes as they recited their vows to each other, ending with a promise to turn two hearts into one.

Wrong DRESS, *Right* GUY

Award-winning author
SHIRLEY HAILSTOCK

Cinnamon Scott can't resist trying on the gorgeous wedding dress mistakenly sent to her. When MacKenzie Grier arrives to retrieve his sister's missing gown, he's floored by this angelic vision...and his own longings. With sparks like these flying, can the altar be far off?

"Shirley Hailstock again displays her tremendous storytelling ability with *My Lover, My Friend.*"
—*Romantic Times BOOKreviews*

Coming the first week of June wherever books are sold.

KIMANI
ROMANCE

"*Obsession* is a five-star delight."
—Harriet Klausner, America On Line Reviewer Board

Essence bestselling author

GWYNNE FORSTER

Obsession

Turning her back on her career, Selena Sutton
settles in a small Texas town where she becomes
entangled in an explosive triangle of desire.
After fighting off the unwanted advances of spoiled
playboy Prince Cooper, she's courted by his brother
Magnus, whose tenderness takes her breath away.
Now the object of both brothers' obsession,
Selena learns the cost of unstoppable passion...
and how priceless true love can be.

*Coming the first week of June
wherever books are sold.*

ARABESQUE®

www.kimanipress.com

KPGF1030608

NATIONAL BESTSELLING AUTHOR

ROCHELLE ALERS

invites you to meet the Whitfields of New York....

Tessa, Faith and Simone Whitfield know all about coordinating
other people's weddings, and not so much about arranging
their own love lives. But in the space of one unforgettable year,
all three will meet intriguing men who just might bring them their
very own happily ever after....

Long Time Coming
June 2008

The Sweetest Temptation
July 2008

Taken by Storm
August 2008

ARABESQUE®

www.kimanipress.com

KPALERSTRIL08

Meet the Whitfield sisters—

experts at coordinating other people's weddings,
but not so great at arranging their own love lives.

NATIONAL BESTSELLING AUTHOR

ROCHELLE ALERS

Long Time Coming

Book #1 of The Whitfield Brides trilogy

When assistant D.A. Micah Sanborn and Tessa Whitfield wind up
stranded together all night in a citywide blackout, they discover a
passion most people only fantasize about. But their romance hits a
snag when Micah is unable to say those three little words.

**Coming the first week of June
wherever books are sold.**

ARABESQUE®

www.kimanipress.com

KPRA0520608